Homecoming
by the Sea

by

Kathi Daley

This book is a work of fiction. Names, characters, places, and incidents either are products of the author's imagination or are used fictitiously. Any resemblance to actual events or locales or persons, living or dead, is entirely coincidental.

Version 1.0

I want to thank the very talented Jessica Fischer for the cover art.

I so appreciate Bruce Curran, who is always ready and willing to answer my cyber questions; Jayme Maness for helping out with the book clubs; and Peggy Hyndman for helping sleuth out those pesky typos.

And, of course, thanks to the readers and bloggers in my life, who make doing what I do possible.

Thank you to Randy Ladenheim-Gil for the editing.

And finally, I want to thank my husband Ken for allowing me time to write by taking care of everything else.

Chapter 1

Monday, May21

I could hear the whispering long before I arrived. It started as a nagging in the back of my mind that grew to a symphony of voices calling me home. I'd felt the echo of what I'd left behind as I made the long trip from one coast to the other.

It had been ten years since I'd stood on this ground. Ten years since I'd heard the voices, felt the connection, seen the images of those who had come before. When I left Cutter's Cove a decade ago, I knew I would return. What I didn't know was how long my return would take.

I stood on the bluff overlooking the angry sea. The sky was dark, with heavy clouds that blocked what was left of the afternoon sun. The rumbling in the distance informed me that a storm was rolling toward shore, but it was the murmurs from the house that caused a chill to run down my spine.

I pulled my sweater tightly around my thin frame as the wind raged from the west. My blond hair blew across my face as I tried to emotionally confront the nightmare that had demanded my return. A good friend had died, brutally murdered in his own home. After six months, his killer still roamed free. This, I'd decided, was something I couldn't bear.

"I'm here," I whispered as the air became heavy with the approaching storm. Lightning flashed across the sky and still I waited. The house had once been my sanctuary, but now, after all this time, I was hesitant to find out who waited impatiently for my return.

I closed my eyes and listened as the waves crashed onto the rocky shore beneath me. I could feel a presence and wondered if my ability to see those who had passed on had been restored now that I'd returned to the house. It wasn't as if I was born with the ability to see ghosts. I hadn't, in fact, seen my first one until I'd moved from New York to Cutter's Cove, Oregon, at the age of sixteen. At the time I believed the gift was the result of some sort of personal growth, but when I moved away from the house and away from the sea, the images faded.

My phone rang, and I turned back toward my Mercedes. I'd promised my mother I'd call when I arrived, so I hurried to the car. I opened the passenger side door and grabbed the phone, which had been resting on the charger.

"Are you there?" Mom asked from the other end of the phone line.

"I'm here."

"How's the house? Ten years is a long time to go without any type of maintenance."

I looked toward the large home that Mom and I had bought and fixed up twelve years ago. We'd found the house—or perhaps the house had found us—during one of the most difficult times in our lives. Spending time together renovating the dilapidated old lady had not only been cathartic but life changing as well. "I haven't been inside, but from the outside she looks just as I remember. She needs a coat of paint, but it seems she's stood strong while she waited."

"Are you sure about this?" Mom asked for the hundredth time.

"I'm sure." I looked out toward the sea. "It's been six months since Booker's death. I spoke to Woody Baker," I said, "and the police are no closer to solving the case than they were on the day his body was found."

"I understand. I really do. But your life is in New York now. Doesn't it feel strange to return to the place where everyone knew you as Alyson?"

I paused before I answered. An image of Alyson flashed through my mind. Although we'd shared the same body, in many ways she felt like a totally different person. When I'd lived in Cutter's Cove a decade ago, I'd used the name Alyson Prescott, a persona I'd been assigned when my mom and I had been placed in the witness protection program. My real name is Amanda Parker, a name I resumed when the men who wanted me dead were murdered themselves. "Yes," I admitted. "It does feel strange. But I have to do this."

"You know I'll support you, whatever you decide."

I smiled. "I know. And I love you for it." I felt a heavy weight settle in my chest. Deciding that serious conversations could wait for another day, I changed the subject. "How's Tucker doing? Didn't he have his checkup today?" Tucker was my German shepherd who stayed with Mom when I went away to college nine years ago. After college I'd secured a high-paying job in a very competitive industry and was rarely home, so Tucker had continued to live with my mother. He was twelve years old now and showing signs of slowing down.

"The vet said he's doing really well for a dog his age. She gave me supplements as well as some mild pain meds to help with the arthritis."

I let out a sigh of relief. "Good. I was worried about him. Give him a kiss for me and tell him I love him."

"Always."

I glanced back toward the house. "I should get inside and try to get the electricity and heat on before the storm arrives. I'm not sure if I'll have reception once it does, so don't worry if you can't get hold of me."

"Okay. Be careful."

I smiled as the reality of my mother's unconditional love warmed my heart. "I will. I love you. I'll call you tomorrow."

I opened the glove box and grabbed the keys to the house. When Mom and I had first come to Cutter's Cove and found the house perched on the edge of the sea, we'd known we were home. Sure, it had stood empty since the death of the previous owner, and admittedly, it had been about as dilapidated as a house could be and still be standing, but it had history and character, and as far as we were concerned, it was love at first sight. Hoping the key would work in the old lock, I slipped it into the door. Luckily, it turned without effort and I stepped inside.

Finally, I heard the house whisper.

I'm not sure how to explain what I felt in that moment. A sense of homecoming, for sure, but also a hollowness I couldn't quite explain. The furniture Mom and I had taken such care to choose was covered with sheets and every other surface was covered with dust. I took a step forward, batting at the tapestry of cobwebs that hung from the ceiling.

I took several more steps into the interior. "Is anyone there?" I said out loud. I hadn't seen anyone, but the sense that I wasn't alone was overwhelming.

As I stood silently and listened, memories I thought long buried suddenly consumed me. When Mom and I had first come to Cutter's Cove I'd been so lost. My best friend had just been murdered and Mom and I had been forced to flee the life we'd always known because the men who'd committed the murder had identified me, the only witness to a gangland shooting. I'd thought leaving Amanda Parker behind would be both painful and confusing, and it was, but I found Alyson's easygoing approach to life surprisingly refreshing. During the two years I'd lived as Alyson, I rarely thought of Amanda, yet it hadn't been all that difficult to reclaim my old life when I returned to the place where Amanda's had been the only identity I'd ever known.

"Is anyone there?" I repeated as I saw a movement out of the corner of my eye.

I paused, but no one answered. I supposed it could just be a trick of the light.

The gas and electrical turnoffs were in the basement, so I headed in that direction. The house was huge and so very different from anything we'd known in New York, with nine fireplaces spread among three floors of living space. There was also a basement and a finished attic. Mom, an artist, had replaced the wall on the ocean side of the attic with windows and had turned the space into a studio. She never spoke of it now that she'd resumed her old life, but I often pictured her there, standing at the window, looking out to sea with a contemplative look on her face.

As I entered the main living area, I glanced at the painting on the wall. Mom had captured me and my two best friends, Mackenzie Reynolds and Trevor Johnson, in an unsuspecting moment and converted the photo to oil. When I'd left Cutter's Cove ten years ago, I'd promised Mac and Trevor that I'd come back to visit all the time. I promised we'd text and Skype every day, and one day find our way back to one another. And we had texted and Skyped. At first. But as the weeks turned into months, and the months into years, we'd become busy with our own lives and drifted apart.

A rustling overhead caused me to pause and listen. It could be animals who'd found their way into the house, though the last time I'd heard strange noises overhead it hadn't been animals at all.

"Hello," I called, louder this time. "Is someone there?"

There was no answer and the rustling stopped, so I continued into the kitchen. I focused on the clickety-clack of my heels hitting the deep blue tile floor as I crossed the room. At the stairs leading down to the basement, I turned on the flashlight on my phone and made my way into the inky darkness of the damp room. When we'd first moved into the house, the space beneath the first floor had been cluttered with remnants from previous residents, as had the attic. Mom and I had cleared out both spaces, and now the basement was mostly empty. My first stop was the electrical box. I'd called the power company a few days before to have the power turned on and hoped all that would be required to bathe the house in light would be a flip of the switch.

"Voilà!" I said as the power came on.

Now all I had to do was turn on the gas and I might be looking at a hot bath that evening. I'd been driving for days, but the journey seemed little more than a blur in my consciousness. Once I'd started the drive west I'd felt the pull of the voices and had thought about little else. After confirming that the gas was working, I went back upstairs to the first floor. It would take me a couple of days of elbow grease before the place was habitable, but for now, I had plumbing and a place to stay. I'd brought an ice chest with a few necessities as well as coffee and wine, so it seemed I could survive the night.

I was about to head upstairs to check out my room when my phone rang. I pulled it out of my pocket and looked at the caller ID. My first reaction was annoyance that my life in New York had found a way to intrude on my first minutes back in Cutter's Cove, then realized how irrational that was and answered. "Ethan. I was just going to call you," I said to my boyfriend of two years, Ethan Wentworth.

"Have you arrived?"

"I have."

"And how did you find it?"

"I mostly remembered how to get here."

Ethan didn't speak for a moment. I knew he was confused by my response, but I couldn't help but tease him after the way he'd framed his question. Ethan was a wonderful person and a kind and considerate boyfriend, but he was a product of old money and a rigid upbringing that resulted in a precise way of moving and speaking.

"I'm just kidding." I laughed. "I found the house to be dusty but intact. How did your court case go?"

"Fine. Our case was impenetrable."

"So you won?"

"Yes. I believe I just said that."

I smiled. "You did, and I'm proud of you. I knew you would tear the place up with your research."

Ethan was a junior partner for one of the top law firms in New York, while I worked as a graphic designer for one of the top advertising agencies.

"Have you had a chance to talk to your policeman friend?" Ethan asked.

"No. I'll track Woody down tomorrow. Right now, I'm exhausted. I just want to settle in, take a hot bath, and maybe have a glass of wine."

"I ran into Skip and Gina today," Ethan said without a beat. He obviously hadn't picked up on my subtle hint that maybe we should sign off now. "They're planning a party next month to celebrate Skip's promotion and their purchase of the new yacht. They asked if you'd be back by then. I told them I thought you would."

I couldn't help but notice his tone made it a question rather than a statement. "I took a six-week leave from the office, but if I get things wrapped up sooner, I'll certainly come home sooner. Still, I don't think I can commit to a party in just a few weeks. I'll have to let you know."

"Are you sure about this venture you've embarked on? You realize it's not your responsibility to find this man's killer."

"Of course it isn't. Still, I think I can help."

"How? I understand he was your friend and his murder has gone unsolved and that makes you sad and angry. But really, Amanda, how can you help?"

I hesitated. Ethan didn't know about my ability to see ghosts. He'd never understand, and I knew I could never tell him. That part of me belonged to Alyson. Ethan was part of Amanda's world. "It's hard to explain. Listen, I have to go. I'll call you tomorrow."

Ethan let out a breath that sounded a lot like frustration. "All right. Be careful."

"I will." I hung up and held the phone to my chest. Ethan didn't understand, and I supposed I didn't blame him. I slipped the phone into my pocket and went toward the stairs. I'd just begun my ascent when a flash of something caught my eye. "Hello," I called once again. "Is someone there?"

There was still no answer, but I was pretty sure what I was seeing and hearing wasn't an animal. "Barkley?" I asked. Barkley Cutter had been the previous owner of the house and the first ghost I'd seen after moving to Cutter's Cove. "Is that you? Are you here?"

There was no answer, but Barkley had never answered in the past. My ability to communicate with ghosts had been limited to seeing them. I'd never been able to speak to them. I was pretty sure Barkley had moved on once my friends and I had solved his murder and found his grandson, so the flash I kept seeing most likely wasn't him.

I supposed any number of spirits could have moved into the house during the decade I'd been gone. In my experience, if they wanted to make contact they would, so I continued to walk on. When I reached the landing to the second floor, I glanced toward the room that had been my mother's. It felt odd to be in the house without her, but she was busy with her new life, or maybe I should say the resumption of her old one. I took a moment to remember the way things had been when we'd first purchased the house, then went to my own room. When I opened the door, I expected to see sheets and cobwebs, as elsewhere, but what I found instead was someone lounging on my bed.

"Who are you?" I asked the apparition, who looked exactly like me. A younger version of me, but me nonetheless.

"I'm Alyson. Who are you?"

"Amanda. What are you?" The form really did look like me, although she was translucent, like a ghost. Somehow, I didn't think she *was* a ghost. For one thing, I wasn't dead. For another, I could speak to her *and* hear her response.

Alyson laid back against the pillow and lifted her legs into the air. She stared at her feet, which were in line with her hips, as if they were the most interesting thing she'd ever seen. "I'm not totally clear on this, but I think I'm the part of you that you left behind."

I narrowed my gaze. "You're part of me? Have you been here this whole time?"

Alyson shrugged. "I guess. What has it been, a couple of weeks?"

"Ten years."

"Damn, girl. I had no idea." Alyson sat up and crossed her legs. "No wonder I'm so bored. Things have been kinda dead around here since you left."

I frowned.

"Get it? Dead around here?" Alyson giggled.

I tossed the Michael Kors bag that held my overnight things on the floor and then sat on the edge of the bed. A white sheet still covered the mattress. "You look like me, but you don't sound like me. I left here when I was seventeen, and even though I was a teenager, I certainly didn't talk or act the way you do."

"What can I say? What you see is the new and improved version of Alyson. Alyson 2.0, if you like."

I frowned. "How is that possible? Even if by some weird chance the part of me that's somehow connected to this house remained behind when I left, why on earth would it have a completely different personality?"

Alyson shrugged. "I guess Amanda took all the stodgy, boring, elitist stuff with her and what was left behind were all the best parts. Did you bring food?"

"Do you eat?"

Alyson's smile faded. "Unfortunately, no. But I can remember what it was like when I was you and you were me and we were one. It's been a while."

"If I eat, will you be able to enjoy it?"

"I have no idea, but I'd love to try." Alyson tilted her head. Her long blond hair swept the mattress. I missed my long hair. At some point along the way I'd decided a woman of my age needed to present a more professional appearance, so I'd cut it. Not super short. Around shoulder length.

I closed my eyes and took several deep breaths. I still wasn't sure if Alyson was real. For all I knew, I was suffering the effects of driving three thousand miles in four days.

"I know what you're thinking," Alyson said. "And I can assure you, I'm real."

I opened my eyes. "How did you know what I was thinking?"

"Duh." Alyson rolled her eyes. "I'm you, remember? And no…" Alyson got up and began jumping up and down on the bed. "You aren't going crazy. And yes, you'll eventually come to love me."

Now I was sure I was having a hallucination. I never jumped on beds as Amanda *or* Alyson. Not even when I was a young child. Jumping on beds was something people like me simply didn't do. "I'm going out to the car to get the rest of my things. I assume you'll be gone when I get back."

Alyson got down off the bed. "Amanda, Amanda, Amanda. How do I make you understand? I'm not going anywhere. I live here. Haven't you been paying attention?"

"I've been paying attention, but that doesn't mean I have to accept what I'm seeing. If you were me, you would act like me. Because you don't, my only conclusion is that you're a figment of my imagination."

Alyson walked over to me. We were exactly the same height, so her blue eyes looked directly into mine. "What happened to you? Don't you remember being Alyson? Don't you remember wearing jeans and going barefoot and having fun? Don't you remember how happy you were once you were able to shed Amanda and her zillions of dollars, private

16

schools, and designer shoes that felt like torture every minute you wore them?"

I glanced down at the pantsuit I was wearing with matching pumps. I really was dying to kick them off and pull on some baggy sweats. Of course, Amanda didn't own baggy sweats. "I do remember," I said. "But that wasn't real. Alyson wasn't real. It was as if I took a vacation from my life, but somewhere inside I knew Amanda was always there, waiting to come out when it was safe to do so."

Alyson shrugged. "Suit yourself. If you're going to empty that fancy car of yours that probably cost more than you paid for this house, you'd better hurry. It's starting to rain."

Ghost me was right. It was starting to rain. I paused for just a moment and then hurried down the stairs to get the things I'd left in my trunk. When I returned, she was gone. Perhaps she'd been an illusion after all.

Chapter 2

Tuesday, May 22

I woke the next morning to sunshine. The storm had come in like a lion, but I was so tired by the time I'd had my bath, slipped into my pajamas, and had a glass of wine, I was out like a light. I'd laid in bed and listened to the waves. I'd missed the way they lulled me to sleep at night. After I'd graduated from college, I'd bought an apartment on the Upper East Side of Manhattan, and most of the time I fell asleep to the sound of the climate control unit that guaranteed a steady temperature switching on and off.

Sitting up, I looked around the room. Still no sign of Alyson. I guess she really had been an illusion. I headed into the bathroom. A hot shower, a cup of coffee, and a bran muffin and I'd be ready to conquer the world. I wanted to track down Woody and grill him for information regarding Booker's murder, but I also wanted to clean up a bit and air out the house.

Booker, whose real name was Rory Oswald, had been gone six months. One more day wouldn't matter.

I thought about the jolly old man I'd grown so fond of during my time in Cutter's Cove. When I met him, he was retired, but he'd donated money to build the most awesome library I'd ever seen in the high school. Well, almost the most awesome. I had, after all, visited the Long Room at Trinity College in Dublin as a child, and if I had to grant the title of most awesome to a library, it would be that one.

It was Booker's own library, however, that had initiated the first visit to his home by the gang and me. We'd been trying to find a buried treasure and hoped he had old journals that would help us solve the riddle with which we'd been presented. Not only had he helped us accomplish our goal, but his enthusiasm had forged a bond between us that had endured until the day I'd left the small seaside town I'd called home for two years for the busy life I'd left behind on the East Coast.

As I stepped into the shower, I found myself glad I'd taken the time to get the gas and electricity going last night. Being able to take a hot shower was going to make all the difference in my day. I felt as if I'd been driving for a lifetime, but it had been only four days. Four *very* long days. I probably should have broken the trip up a bit, but once I'd made the decision to come to Cutter's Cove, I'd become impatient to be there.

I turned off the water, pulled back the shower curtain, and reached for a towel on the rack next to the shower when Alyson appeared. I let out an involuntary screech. "You scared the heck out of me." I pulled the shower curtain in front of me.

"Sorry." Alyson giggled. "I've been waiting for you to get up. Did you know you snore?"

"I most certainly do not snore." I wrapped the towel around my body.

Alyson shrugged. "Whatever you say. What are we going to do today?"

"Do?"

"I haven't been out in forever and I'm pretty sure if you go out, I can go with you."

"If you can go with me, why did you stay behind when I went back to New York?" I wrapped a hand towel around my hair.

"Maybe I should clarify. I can go with you as long as you're living in this house. It's to the house I'm bonded. Can we have pancakes for breakfast?"

I pulled on a robe and began drying my hair. "Pancakes are fattening."

"But we're skinny. Please?"

I turned off the hair dryer and looked at what I was sure was a hallucination. "Pancakes spike my blood sugar and then I'm hungry again an hour later. Besides, I haven't been to the store yet, so I don't have the ingredients for pancakes. I brought some bran muffins with me."

"Bran muffins are for when you're old and irregular." Alyson paused. "Is that it? Are you irregular from the trip?"

"No, I'm not irregular." I put my hand on my hip. "Now, if you don't mind, I'd like to finish getting ready. Alone," I emphasized.

"If I leave you alone, can we go into town and get pancakes?"

She certainly was persistent. Maybe there was a part of me inside her after all. I groaned in frustration.

"Fine. Whatever it takes to dry my hair without interruption."

Alyson disappeared as abruptly as she'd appeared. There was no doubt about it: I was totally losing my mind.

I dried my hair, then used my curling iron to shape it and applied my makeup. It hadn't been my plan to go into town today, but I did need to buy some groceries, and it wouldn't hurt to visit my old friend, Chan, to find out what in the heck was going on with my annoying shadow. Chan owned a magic shop and had helped us out with all things mystical on a number of occasions. Maybe he would not only know what was going on but how to fix it.

After dressing in a pair of designer slacks, a silk blouse, and low-heeled pumps, I headed downstairs, where I found Alyson waiting near the door. "Is that what you're wearing to get pancakes?" she asked.

I looked down at my clothes. "What's wrong with what I'm wearing?"

"It's so... so ..." Alyson threw her hands into the air. "I can't think of a way to finish that sentence that wouldn't be rude. Let's go before you change your mind."

I picked up my purse and headed out to my car. Alyson appeared in the passenger seat after I climbed into the driver's seat. I clasped my seat belt and adjusted the mirror. "Buckle up," I instructed.

"Really?" Alyson looked at me with a raised eyebrow.

"Yeah, okay. I guess that isn't necessary. So, where do you want to go for pancakes?"

"Mom always made the best pancakes, but I guess popping over for a visit isn't in the cards. How about that breakfast place downtown? Felicia's?"

"The one with the red-and-white awning?"

"Sounds right."

I started the car and pulled onto the private road that led out to the highway. This really was the most bizarre morning I'd had for quite some time. "Do you like music?" I asked as I reached for the radio.

"I'm you. If you like music, I like music."

"If that's true, why are we going for pancakes? It seems if I like bran muffins, you should like them too."

"You don't like bran muffins. You've compared them to eating sawdust. You only eat them because you think you should. You do, however, like pancakes. You just won't let yourself have them."

I supposed Alyson had a point; I did prefer pancakes to bran muffins. Still, if I let her make all the decisions, I was going to end up weighing two hundred pounds before this visit was over.

I pulled up in front of Felicia's and got out. Luckily, a table was open near the window. It felt friendly and nostalgic, being back in a place that, before today, had seemed more like a dream than a memory. I ordered a cup of coffee and a short stack of pancakes. Once they were in front of me, I buttered them and poured the warm maple syrup over the top.

"Um. These really are delicious," I said after taking my first bite. "I haven't had pancakes for years. I'm glad you badgered me into this."

"You might not want to talk to me when we aren't alone," Alyson suggested.

I looked around the room. Everyone was staring at me. Of course, I was the only one who could see ghost me. I smiled at the woman in the booth closest to me, then took a sip of my coffee.

"I can taste the sweetness," Alyson said. "Apparently, whatever you eat, I can experience. Can we have pizza for lunch?"

"We'll see," I said, before I had time to monitor myself. There was no doubt about it: a stop at Chan's was an absolute next on the agenda. If Alyson and I really had become fragmented, there had to be a way to slap us back together again.

******

The magic shop, in the oldest section of downtown Cutter's Cove, featured white curtains framing a large picture window on the outside. Inside, shelves of books as well as glass jars filled with all sorts of strange-looking things, including eye of newt and frog legs, drew me in and reawakened my curiosity. But I wasn't here to shop. Today I was here for answers.

"Amanda; Alyson," greeted Chan, a small Asian man who seemed to glide in the air from out of nowhere. "I've been expecting you."

"It's good to see you." I smiled at the mysterious man who seemed to know everything.

"I've prepared tea." Chan locked the front door and changed the "Open" sign to "Closed." "Let's go in the back and we can chat."

We followed Chan down the hallway I'd traveled many times before. We entered the room he used for rest and meditation, and I sat down on one of the large pillows while he poured us each a cup of the tea he had somehow known to prepare.

"I guess you know I'm here to ask about Alyson." I angled my head toward ghost me, who was examining a jar of eyeballs. "I was quite surprised to find her in my bedroom when I arrived at the house last night."

"Alyson is the part of you that is attached to the house."

"Told you," Alyson said, a grin on her face.

"Yes, she informed me of that. And I guess I sort of understand. I do have questions, though. For one thing, why is she so different from me?"

Chan took a sip of his tea before answering. "Alyson is the part of you that you shed when you left Cutter's Cove for New York. She is the part you felt would not fit into your old life. She is the part who possesses an innocent heart and an ability to suspend disbelief. She is the part of you where magic lives."

I took a sip of my own tea. Orange spice; my favorite. "I see." I glanced at Alyson, who looked content. "What I really need to know is how to get her back on the inside. It's a little unnerving, having her running around on the outside."

"Hey, I'm right here," Alyson complained. "No need to talk about me like I can't hear what you're saying."

I turned and smiled at ghost me. "I'm sorry. I guess that *was* rude." I turned back to Chan. "Can you help me?"

"It is up to you to reunite the two parts. When you are ready to allow Alyson in, the two parts will be whole again."

"Let her in? What do you mean?"

Chan smiled. "It is not for me to say."

"How will I know if I've been successful?" I asked.

Alyson rolled her eyes. "'Cause if you've been successful I'll be tagging along on the inside, not the outside."

I looked at Chan. "Are you sure Alyson is really an aspect of me? She seems so different. Not just because she seems to have been stuck in some sort of eternal teenage persona, but even at that age I wasn't quite so…"

"Fun?" Alyson provided.

"Silly," I corrected.

Chan chuckled. "I can assure you, Amanda, Alyson is as much a part of you as any other aspect."

As usual, I left Chan's with more questions than answers. It would seem I'd stop coming to him for help, although if I were honest, he always did seem to have the answers, even if it seemed to take me quite a lot of time to understand what he was saying.

"So, can we have pizza?" Alyson asked.

"We just had pancakes."

"We ate like three bites. Please. Just a slice."

I let out a breath and agreed. I supposed a slice wouldn't hurt, and I'd been craving Pirates Pizza since the moment I crossed the Oregon state line. It not only had the best pizza in town, it had the best pizza anywhere.

It was early for lunch, so the place was mostly deserted when we walked in. I took a deep breath of delicious goodness as I walked up to the hostess desk.

"I'll be right there," someone called from the kitchen. "Go ahead and take a seat anywhere."

"Trevor?"

A tall man with dark brown hair and a boyish grin popped his head out the door of the kitchen. "Alyson?"

"I go by Amanda now, but yes."

"Well I'll be." Trevor crossed the place and lifted me into his arms. Alyson laughed with glee as he spun me around and around. "I can't believe you're actually standing here in my pizza joint."

"Not standing. Spinning," I corrected.

"Sorry." Trevor stopped spinning and set me on the floor in front of him. "I just can't believe you're here. You cut your hair."

I put a hand to my shoulder-length hair. "Yes. Quite a while ago."

"It looks good. Different, but good. How's the job? Are you still working for that magazine?"

"I'm a graphic designer for an advertising agency now. The job requires long hours, but I like the creative outlet it provides."

"So, you're still in New York?"

I nodded.

Trevor lowered his eyes. "It sounds as if you aren't here to stay."

"I'm just here for a few weeks. Or really, as long as it takes."

"Takes for what?" Trevor asked.

"I came to find Booker's killer."

Trevor took my arm and led me to a booth. "I'm so glad you're here and so glad to hear you say that. I can't believe someone would kill that sweet old man. I've talked to Woody about it, but he's totally stumped. I've been wishing you were here, and now you are."

I smiled. "I guess wishes do come true."

"Absolutely. Now that you're here, we'll finally get some answers. We need to call Mac. It's time to get the Scooby gang back together."

"Is Mac in town?" I asked.

"No. She works for a big tech firm in California. We chat on the phone or by Skype a couple of times a week, and we've discussed the Booker thing several times. She even suggested the two of us should look in to it. It seemed sort of pointless without you. But now that you're committed, I know we'll finally bring Booker's killer to justice." Trevor took out his phone. "I'll call her." He took a couple of steps away to make his call.

I'd met Trevor and Mac on my first day of school in Cutter's Cove. To say I was like a fish out of water there would be putting it mildly. I'd grown up in a family from old money with old-world ideas. I spent my summers in the Hamptons, vacationed in Europe, lived in a penthouse apartment, partied with the wealthy, and attended an exclusive, expensive private girl's school. The minute I arrived in Cutter's Cove, I became a middle-class girl living a middle-class life. They'd taken me under their wing, becoming instant friends who'd shown me the ropes, taken me to my first football game, and taught me how much fun life could be in a small town.

"Don't forget the pizza," Alyson said as Trevor prepared to hang up.

"I won't forget."

"Won't forget what?" Trevor asked.

"Pizza. I've been dreaming about it for three thousand miles. Why are you here exactly?"

"I own the place."

"Own it?" I'm not sure why that surprised me, but it did. In high school, Trevor had been the most popular boy on campus. He was funny and friendly, as well as being the quarterback for the football team and the shooting guard for the basketball team. To top it all off, he was exceptionally good-looking, which made most of the girls swoon whenever he paid them any attention. What he hadn't been was academically ambitious.

"I bought it five years ago. I thought I might have mentioned it."

I didn't respond because Trevor and I both knew we hadn't talked about anything much in the past five years. My fault, not his. He'd tried to keep the long-distance friendship going; I'd been the one who let it die.

"So, is Mac on board?"

"She said she'll be on the next flight north. She'll fly into Portland and rent a car. Should we meet this evening?"

I made a quick decision. "We should. I'm staying at the house. Why don't you and Mac come over when she gets here?"

"I'll bring pizza." Trevor hugged me again. "I really can't tell you how happy I am to see you."

Trevor and I took a few minutes to catch up before the lunch crowd began to arrive. I didn't need pizza for lunch if we were having it for dinner, and Alyson didn't argue. After saying a temporary good-bye to Trevor, I left the pizza parlor and went out to the car.

"I should go to the grocery store. I know Trevor said he'd bring pizza, but that won't fill him up for very long."

"I've really missed him," Alyson said.

"Yeah." I choked back a tear. "Me too."

"He looked good. Really good."

"He did," I agreed.

"He still has the same boyish good looks, but he's filled out in a very nice way. He's quite the babe, don't you think?" Alyson asked.

I adjusted my visor. "I guess. I didn't really notice."

"Liar. I'm you, remember. If my heart beat just a tiny bit faster when he kissed us good-bye, yours did too."

"I have a boyfriend back in New York," I reminded ghost me.

"Yes, you have a boyfriend back in New York. I'm on the market."

I laughed out loud. "Do you have any idea how insane this sounds?"

Alyson giggled. "Yeah. I'm having fun too."

I turned up the music and rolled down the windows. I never drove with the windows down back home. In fact, this might very well be the first time the windows had been down on this car, which I'd only had a few months.

"Do you think we should go talk to Woody now?" Alyson asked.

"It'll be a good idea to find out what he knows before we get together tonight."

"Do you think he still smiles with his eyes?" Alyson wondered.

I shrugged. "He might."

I'd first met Woody when I was about to start my senior year of high school. We were trying to solve a murder that had taken place a decade before, and he'd been a brand-new cop on the force, so he hadn't developed the hard shell a lot of cops eventually do. He had a friendly smile and huge brown eyes, and I'll admit to having a bit of a crush on him. I wasn't quite as giddy as Alyson, but I was looking forward to seeing him again.

"Well, if it isn't Alyson Prescott," Woody said, and wrapped me in a big hug.

"I'm Amanda now." I hugged him back.

Woody took a step back. "Except for the hair and stylish clothes, you look just the same."

I looked up at the twinkle in his eyes. "Thank you. Time has been kind to you as well."

"I guess you're here to talk about your friend's murder."

I nodded. "I've come three thousand miles to try to help figure this out. I only hope I haven't lost my knack over the years."

"I only have a few minutes to talk now—I have an appointment across town in less than thirty minutes—but I can fill you in briefly. Come on back to my office."

I followed Woody down the hall. He motioned for me to take a seat across the desk from him. He logged into his computer and opened a file. "If I had more time I could go into specifics, but all I can do right now is go over the basics."

"That's fine," I said. "A basic understanding of what occurred and a place to start will be fine."

Woody fixed his eyes on the screen and began to read. "Rory Oswald, better known as Booker, was found dead in his home on the morning of November 10 by his housekeeper, Marina Parish. Ms. Parish found Mr. Oswald on the floor of the library when she went in to clean. The medical examiner found that Mr. Oswald had been dead for about twelve hours by the time Ms. Parish stumbled onto him. He died of a single gunshot wound to the back.'"

I cringed. I couldn't help it. I was squeamish, and the thought of Booker being brutally murdered was more than I thought I could take. "So you don't have any suspects?"

"I didn't say that. On the surface, there didn't seem to be a single one, but given that he was found in the library near the bookshelves, I began to suspect someone was after something Booker had in that room. Perhaps information. If you remember, he had an extensive library that contained a lot of old documents and journals as well as books. My best guess is that he was forced at gunpoint to provide the attacker with whatever he was after; then, when the attacker had what he was after, he shot him."

I bowed my head. I'd known before I got there how Booker had died, but discussing it with someone who'd seen the crime scene made it seem that much more real. "Was there anything in the library that narrowed things down at all?"

"The crime scene guys went over the house from top to bottom. They didn't find any evidence that would point to any specific person, but we assumed it was someone he knew because there was no sign of a forced entry. We pulled dozens of fingerprints from the house, but none seemed particularly suspect."

"Has anyone come forward to offer a theory or explanation of who might have wanted him dead?"

Woody swiped his dark hair, which grew long in the front, from his eyes. "No, not really. We always receive a bunch of anonymous tips in cases like this, but nothing has panned out." He sat back in his chair. "I know the two of you were close. And I know you've come a long way to find Mr. Oswald's killer. But I have to be honest: the well seems to have run dry. We've investigated every lead no matter how slight and come up empty."

I leaned my head back and stared at the ceiling. I fought the tears that wanted to escape as I tried to formulate a coherent response. After a moment, I lowered my head and looked at Woody. "I know you've done the best you could. And I appreciate it. And I don't know if I'll have any more success than you have. But I have to try. I hope you understand."

"I do. And I remember the success you had with seemingly impossible cases when you were in high school. I'd be foolish to send you away. What do you need?"

"Copies of everything you have would help. Mac's coming from California and Trevor's closing Pirates Pizza early. We're meeting at my house at seven."

Woody took a minute before answering. "I'll provide the copies, but only if you include me in the discussion. I realize I've come up empty so far, but this is still an open investigation. An official presence would be a good idea."

"Okay," I agreed. "I'll see you at seven. Bring beer."

After we left the police station I found myself saying to myself—and Alyson— "I wonder if we should bother to go to the store now. I suppose we can just go later."

Alyson shook her head. "We need to go now. We need cat food."

"Cat food? We don't have a cat."

"Sure we do. Don't you remember Shadow?"

I did remember Shadow. He was a large black cat that had come into my life when I'd been in hiding on Madrona Island. He, like me, had the ability to see those who had passed on, and in some sort of strange but wonderful way, it quickly became apparent we were somehow connected. When I left Madrona Island and returned to Cutter's Cove, he'd come with me. Before I left Cutter's Cove, he'd disappeared. I'd looked and looked for him, but now I thought he must have preferred to stay behind.

"Shadow is still here?" I asked.

Alyson smiled. "Of course. He's bonded to us, as is the house. He'll be glad you're home. He's had to fend for himself since you've been gone. It's not like I could go to the store to buy cat food."

"Why didn't I see him yesterday?" I asked. "Or this morning?"

Alyson shrugged. "He comes and goes. He's home now. I can sense him."

I smiled. It would be good to see him again. I'd thought of him often, wondering many times what had become of him. "Okay. Then I'll go to the store now. If I'm going to have guests, I should buy some snacks and beverages anyway."

"Don't forget ice cream. We love ice cream," Alyson reminded me.

I laughed. "We do love ice cream.

"Eaten straight from the carton," we said at the same time.

Chapter 3

When the black BMW pulled into the drive, I thought it might belong to someone who was lost. When I opened the front door and found Alyson jumping around in unbridled excitement, I knew it was Mac. I wanted to join Alyson in her happy dance, but Amanda didn't jump around like a lunatic no matter how happy she was. Instead, I stepped out onto the front porch and waited.

"You really are here?" Mac shouted as she opened the driver's door and stepped out. I opened my arms to her as she flew from the drive onto the porch.

"I missed you so much," Mac said as she hugged me so tightly I could barely breathe.

"I missed you too." I hugged her back. Until this moment, I hadn't known just how much I'd missed her.

"When Trev called and said you were here, I wasn't sure I believed him." Mac took a step back. There were tears streaming down her face. "I thought we'd never see you again."

I didn't know what to say. There was nothing *to* say. I'd had the best friends in the entire world and I'd let them fade away. "You look exactly the same," I eventually murmured.

Mac looked me up and down, frowned, and then smiled. "And you look different. Good. But different."

I put a hand to my shoulder-length hair before looking down at my slacks, silk blouse, and low heels. "You used to know Alyson. Today you're seeing Amanda." I looked at Mac. "I know that's a weird thing to say. But I missed you and I'm so happy you're here now."

"Not as happy as me." Mac wiped the tears from her cheeks with the back of her hand.

"Are you staying with your parents?"

Mac shook her head. "The family moved to Tucson years ago."

"Then you'll stay with me. It's dusty but livable. Let's get your things."

Mac nodded and then looked down to my feet. "Is that Shadow?"

I picked up the furry black cat. "Yes, it's Shadow. Can you believe he was here waiting for me?"

"Actually, no. He looks just the same. It's like he didn't age at all while you were gone."

I shrugged. "We both know he's some sort of magical kitty. I guess magic cats don't age. To be honest, I was so thrilled to see him, I didn't even stop to wonder at the specifics."

Mac reached out a hand to pet the cat. "And Tucker?"

"He lives with my mom. Unlike Shadow, he aged. He's been with my mom for quite a while, but I see him all the time."

"I remember the day you got him. He was all legs and ears. I can't believe it's been twelve years."

Yeah, me neither, I thought to myself as I set Shadow on the ground and followed Mac out to her car. I hadn't had a lot of time to clean, but I'd removed the sheets from the furniture in the living room and run a dustcloth around until it looked somewhat decent. I'd cleaned my bedroom and bathroom as well but hadn't gotten around to any of the guest rooms. Mac didn't seem to mind the dust, so we put her things in the room across the hall from mine.

"So, tell me everything," Mac said after we'd dropped off her luggage and returned downstairs.

I paused. Where would I even start? It both felt like I'd been gone a lifetime and like I'd been gone only a few minutes.

"Start at the beginning. Tell her how hard it was to leave and what you've done since," Alyson suggested. "But keep it short. The guys will be here soon."

"There's a lot to tell and no way I can tell you everything in a few short minutes," I finally answered. "We have a lot of time to catch up on. What I do want to say now is that I'm sorry. I'm sorry I didn't keep my promise to stay in touch and I'm sorry I let the friendship we had fade away."

"Why did you?" Mac asked, a serious expression on her face.

I took a deep breath. "I think the day Mom and I drove out of town was the hardest of my life. I'd been through a lot of hard things in my life, more than anyone should have to go through, but leaving you and Trevor and my life here was almost unbearable. I wanted to stay, but I knew my mom wanted to return to what she'd left behind. She'd given up so much for me: her family, her career, her friends, her marriage. I couldn't ask her to stay once the danger was over, so I agreed to go. I really thought I'd finish high school and come back."

"But things changed," Mac prompted.

I nodded. "The longer I was away from my life here, the easier it was to be Amanda. It was almost like I left Alyson behind, and the longer I was separated from her, the less real she seemed. I didn't set out to hurt you and Trevor. You meant so much to me. But the days passed, and I went to college and started a career and fell in love, and my life as Alyson seemed like nothing more than a nice memory."

"Fell in love?"

I should have known Mac would pick up on that. "His name is Ethan. He's a junior partner in a law firm and we've been together for two years."

"Any wedding plans?"

I paused. "No. He's busy with his career and I'm busy with mine. What we have suits us."

"I see."

I could tell by the look on Mac's face that she really didn't. "How about you? Any men in your life worth talking about?"

Mac shook her head. "Not right now. I tend to get antsy after I've been in a relationship for a while, so I have a history of breaking things off before they get too complicated. I've had a few long-term relationships I hoped would go the distance, but none seemed exactly right. I'm not sure happily ever after is in the cards for me. I tend to be particular about who I spend my time with. If I really think about it, you and Trev are the only people I've ever been interested in maintaining a relationship with for the long haul. And my family, of course. And your mom. How's your mom?" Mac asked.

"She's good. She reopened her gallery and rekindled a lot of her old friendships. She has a wonderful estate in Bronxville. It's close to the city, which allows her to keep up with her art gallery and her charity work, but it's far enough from the hustle and bustle to provide a quiet, more laid-back lifestyle."

"And your dad?"

I shrugged. "I see him, but not all that often."

"He didn't reconcile with your mom when you got home?"

My father had chosen to divorce my mother rather than come with us when we were relocated. "He made his choice. My mom is happy. I don't think she regrets that they're no longer together." That still made me feel sad and guilty. "How about you? Other than not becoming seriously involved in a romantic relationship, what have you been up to?"

"College, computers, world domination. You know; same old, same old."

I laughed. "I don't doubt any of it. You were and still are the smartest person I know. Do you like your job?"

Mac lifted one shoulder. "Eh."

"*Eh* doesn't sound good."

"*Eh* is fine. *Eh* makes me a boatload of money. *Eh* provides me with the opportunity to work with people

I like and admire. But it's grown to be somewhat predictable. The excitement is gone. I think it might be time for a change."

"Are you going to break up with your job?"

Mac laughed. "I think it might be time."

"Do you have something else in mind?"

Mac tilted her head of curly red hair. "I'm thinking of starting my own company. Cybersecurity is all the rage, and it might be a lot more interesting than developing business software."

"Wow. That's great, Mac." I leaned forward and hugged her. "I'm incredibly happy for you. I knew from the moment I met you that you were destined for great things."

I watched as Alyson flew to the front door and plastered her face to the window. "It sounds like the guys are here," I said based on her actions. Was I really that boy crazy when I was a teen? I didn't think so. Of course, Alyson wasn't really me, only a part of me. From my observation, she wasn't only the fun part but the hormonal part as well.

******

"So, tell me what Booker was up to in the days preceding his death," I said later that evening, after the pizza had been devoured. I was giddy with happiness that my friends and I were together again, but I really wanted to find Booker's killer.

"In the days right before, Booker was busy working on the new wing he'd donated to the history museum," Trevor said.

"He donated a whole wing?" I asked.

"He did," Woody confirmed. "I imagine he realized he was getting on in years and was thinking about leaving a legacy behind. He spoke to Caleb Wellington and they came up with the idea of adding a wing to the museum in his name."

"Caleb is back in town?" When I'd left Cutter's Cove, I hadn't been the only one heading to New York.

"He is," Trevor answered my question. "He's not only a very active member of the historical society but he's opened an art gallery in town. He does very well for himself, not that he needs the money."

"Wow," I said. "I'm looking forward to reconnecting. But go on with your story." I looked at Woody, then Trevor. "Both of you."

"The wing he donated focuses on shipping in the area, and how the cargo ships that ran up and down the West Coast from South America to Alaska helped to carve out local history," Woody continued. "Mr. Oswald had a lot of information about the subject and the role it played in the development of Cutter's Cove, and he donated a lot of old artifacts. The historical society put out a call for additional donations, much the same as they did when the museum was first founded."

I did remember that. My mother had helped Caleb open the museum in the beginning.

"A couple of boxes of items were donated that seemed to be of special interest to Mr. Oswald," Woody said. "He didn't want to say exactly why he found the boxes of dishes and pipes so fascinating, but he did request that he be given the chance to look at everything before it was displayed."

"Did you ever find out why he was so excited about the dishes?" I asked.

"After his death, I interviewed his friends, as well as the people who worked and volunteered at the museum. I specifically asked if they knew why the dishes and pipes had him so excited. One of the volunteers, a woman named Gilda Joffrey, told me that she'd spoken to Booker about them. She's a retired history professor, so they had some interests in common and had become friends. She said Mr. Oswald believed the things in the boxes were part of the cargo of the *Santa Isabella*."

"Sounds like a treasure hunt." Trevor rubbed his hands together.

"Perhaps," Woody acknowledged. "According to Ms. Joffrey, the *Santa Isabella* was a cargo ship that traveled between South America and San Francisco in the mid-eighteen hundreds. She was heading north with a full load when she disappeared. No one knows for sure what happened to her, but Ms. Joffrey told me that Booker had long held the theory that the ship had ended up at the bottom of the sea just off our coast."

"Why would it have been so far off route?" I asked Woody.

"Apparently, Booker had several theories, but he didn't know for certain. He suspected she may have been blown off course after encountering a storm, or she could have been captured by pirates who brought the ship north, offloaded the cargo, and then sank her, or it was even possible, to his mind, that the crew brought the ship north, stole the cargo, and then sank it. Booker is the only one who really knows why he was so certain the ship sank in this area; I'm afraid that's something he'll never be able to tell us now."

"Okay, so Booker had theories about why the ship would have been this far north, but my question is, why did he think the ship sank here and not somewhere between South America and San Francisco?" Mac asked.

"From what I understand, Booker found a couple dozen gold buckles on the beach after a huge storm several decades ago. The buckles were custom made, and Booker thought they were part of the cargo of the *Santa Isabella*. Again, only Booker really knows why he found these buckles so important."

I sat back and let this sink in. The room was quiet until I spoke. "Okay, Booker finds these gold buckles and decides to research them. He finds out they resemble buckles that were described as part of the cargo of a ship that should never have been this far north in the first place. That piques his interest, so he continues to research the matter, finally settling on the theory that for whatever reason, the ship sank off this coast. If I know Booker, he was probably researching it ever since."

"Sounds about right," Woody confirmed.

"And when other items he suspected were part of the cargo of the *Santa Isabella* are donated to the museum, he realizes this could serve as proof his theory was correct," Mac added.

Woody nodded. "Without having spoken to Mr. Oswald about it, it's impossible to know what he was thinking for sure, but if Ms. Joffrey is correct in her assumption that he was on to something, then yes, I believe he could have seen the donated items as some sort of proof of his theory."

"Other than buckles, dishes, and pipes, what else was the ship carrying?" Trevor asked.

"The *Santa Isabella* was a merchant ship, so when I asked Ms. Joffrey that same question, she said it was likely that much of the cargo was perishable. The ship would likely have been transporting coffee, tobacco, silks, and slaves, among other things. All those items would have disappeared long ago. The things that would survive under the right circumstances— pottery, crystal, gold buckles, and porcelain pipes— would be the proof Mr. Oswald needed."

"Maybe, but pottery, buckles, and pipes from a century ago would have some value in this day and age, though they don't sound like the kinds of things one would kill over," I replied.

"Maybe the ship also carried gold and jewels," Trevor said.

"Ms. Joffrey seemed to think that was unlikely," Woody replied.

"Are we thinking Booker's interest in the cargo is what led to his death?" I asked.

"I have no idea." Woody's voice clearly demonstrated his frustration. "All I know for sure is that on the night he died, Mr. Oswald was at a party. Other guests reported that he got a text about halfway through the evening and left. No one I spoke to saw him alive again. According to the medical examiner, he would have died between one and three hours after he left the party."

"Whoever texted him probably killed him," I said. It seemed this mystery might be easier to solve than I thought.

"Probably. The problem is, Mr. Oswald didn't receive the text on his own phone. Or at least not on the phone he used every day. We found that one in his pocket, but there was no evidence of his receiving any texts on it that night. My theory is that Mr. Oswald had a second phone with him at the party. I haven't found any evidence that a second phone was registered to him, so I imagine it must have been a burner phone, perhaps carried that night for the express purpose of receiving the text. So far, we haven't been able to find a second phone if one did exist."

"Bummer," Alyson said.

I sent her a meaningful glance. I didn't think anyone else could hear or see her, but you could never be too careful. The last thing I needed was everyone thinking I had completely lost my mind.

"Did any of the staff at Booker's house see anything?" I asked.

"No one was on the property when the murder occurred. I interviewed the woman who found the body, Marina Parish, and the groundskeeper, José Montoya. Neither had anything to offer."

We were all quiet after that, as we took a moment to let everything sink in. Eventually, Mac asked if we could take a look in Booker's house.

"I think that can be arranged. Booker left his home and the grounds on which it stands to the historical society. His niece was named as the caregiver, and she's living there now. Her name is Monica."

"We know Monica," Trevor said. "We all went to high school together. I didn't even know she was still in town."

"She wasn't prior to her uncle's death." Woody's phone beeped, and he frowned. He pulled it out of his pocket and looked at the message. "I'm sorry, but I need to go. There's been an accident on the highway."

Chapter 4

For the first time in a long time it was just us, the Scooby gang. "What do you think?" I asked the others.

"I think Booker was a smart man with a lot of resources," Trevor said. "And we all know he enjoyed a treasure hunt as much as anyone. I bet he figured out what happened to the *Santa Isabella* and either found more of the cargo or figured out where to start looking for it."

"We need to find out what Booker knew," Mac suggested. "If we can get into his home maybe we can find something on his computer or in his safe."

"I'm sure the police have already looked in both those places," I pointed out.

"Maybe. But they might not know about Booker's secret hiding place in the stacks."

Mac was right. They probably wouldn't know about that. Maybe we'd be able to find whatever it was that had gotten Booker killed.

I sat back on the sofa and crossed my legs beneath me. "Let's take a look at Woody's report. The first thing we need to do is figure out what ground he's already covered. And then we should get up to speed with the *Santa Isabella* and the things that were donated to the museum. I'd like to speak to whoever donated them as well. Do we know who that is?"

Trevor picked up the folder and began to thumb through it. He picked up a sheet of paper and began to scan it. "This says the items were donated to the museum by Illia Powell, who found the boxes in her mother's attic after she passed away. She didn't know how long the boxes had been there, but the house had been in the family for four generations. It was built by her great-grandfather in 1910 and was passed down to her grandfather, who left it to her mother. Now it's hers."

"Does Ms. Powell live in town?" I asked.

Trevor shrugged. "It doesn't say, but there's a phone number. I guess we can call her tomorrow."

"What else does Woody have in the file?" I asked.

He thumbed through it. "It looks like he has interview notes on four, no wait, five people. I'll read out what Woody has, and Mac can take notes. She'll want to dig around into the background of anyone we suspect."

It was sort of odd to find Trevor taking the lead. Years ago, he'd mostly hung back. Of course, he was twenty-seven now and not seventeen, and he owned his own business.

"First up are the notes from his interview with Gilda Joffrey; next we have notes relating to an interview with Walter Brown." Trevor looked up from the file. "I know Walter. He's a retired doctor who keeps busy by volunteering. He joined the board of the historical society about four years ago. He's friendly and well liked, and I know he and Booker were friends."

Mac made a few notes on her laptop while I just watched, soaking in the excitement of having a new mystery to solve. I'd really missed it. "Why did Woody interview him?"

Trevor looked down at the report. "It looks like he asked Walter about the items that were donated. Booker hadn't mentioned why he was so interested in the boxes of dishes and pipes, so it appears he didn't take Walter into his confidence the way he had Ms. Joffrey. Woody asked the standard questions relating to possible motive and Walter said he couldn't think of a single person who would want to hurt him."

"Anything else?"

Trevor shook his head. "Not really. I don't think Walter was considered a suspect, just a source of information, given his friendship with Booker."

I took a sip of water from the bottle I always kept nearby. "Who else did Woody talk to?" I glanced at Mac, who continued to keyboard.

"The third set of interview notes are from a man named James Hornsby. He's retired and, like Walter, fills his days doing volunteer work. Before moving to Cutter's Cove, he was a pharmacist in Portland. He works two days a week at the museum, and while I don't think he was as close to Booker as Gilda and Walter, they knew each other."

I tried not to stare at Alyson, who had suddenly materialized and was sitting so close to Trevor that she appeared to be almost sitting on his lap. I jerked my head to the right, hoping she'd pick up on my cue to move over, but she ignored me, proving that it really was possible not to pay any attention to yourself. "Go on," I encouraged.

"Hornsby said he didn't know anything about the things that had been donated or why Booker might have been interested in them. He did say he and Booker played in the same poker game from time to time, and he'd seen a man named Logan Poland threaten Booker when he cleaned him out with a straight flush. Poland swore no one was as lucky as Booker was that evening, so he was convinced he had to be cheating. Booker insisted he had no need to cheat and refused to be pulled into the argument or to defend himself. That seemed to make Poland even madder. Eventually, he left, but on his way out, Hornsby heard him muttering under his breath that he was going to get even with Booker." Trevor frowned and looked up. "The poker game took place two days before Booker was shot."

"Did Woody interview Poland?" I asked.

"Hang on." Trevor shuffled through the report, which was several pages long. "There's just a note that one of the other officers verified Poland's alibi for the night of the murder." Trevor looked up. "I guess we should ask Woody about that."

"Yes, I will," I said.

"The next set of interview notes come from Woody's interview with Sam Sutton," Trevor went on.

"Why does that name sound familiar?" I asked.

Trevor looked up from the file. "He used to work for Mayor Gregor back when you lived here."

"That's right. He was some sort of an assistant. I can't believe he stayed here after everything that happened." Gregor had been caught up in some dirty dealing and had been killed because of it.

"Sam is an okay guy," Trevor responded. "He moved away for a while after the mayor died, but then he came back and opened a hardware store. He still works the counter five days a week."

"Okay; I look forward to seeing him," I responded. "So why did Woody talk to him?"

"Booker had hired Sam to oversee some maintenance on his house; he'd just started to offer the service as an add-on to the hardware store. Sam had Carter Carson do the actual repairs, which were fairly minor but too much for a man of Booker's age."

"What sort of repairs?" I asked.

Trevor looked up. "Woody's notes don't say, but one of my waitresses hired Sam to do some light maintenance at her place. Things like changing the heater filter as well as the batteries in the smoke detectors. I guess Woody was interested in speaking to Sam because his employee would have been working inside Booker's house the week before he died."

"Did Sam know anything?"

Trevor looked at the notes once again. "It doesn't look like it." He frowned. "It seems he should have spoken to Carter rather than Sam, though."

"I'll ask him about that as well," I said. "Anyone else in the file?"

"Chelsea Green."

My mouth fell open. "Chelsea Green, the homecoming queen who made my life difficult for two years?"

Trevor nodded. "Chelsea went away to college but quit after her junior year. She moved back in with her parents but wanted her own place. Her father said he'd pay for an apartment if she got a job. It just so happened they had an opening at the museum."

I frowned. "An opening? What does Chelsea do?"

"She greets people, answers questions, conducts tours. She's actually very good at it. In fact, since she's become the face of the museum, the annual donations have tripled. She's even planning a gala to kick off the new wing Booker donated. Chelsea was pretty clueless when she was in high school, but she's liked and respected by most of the people in Cutter's Cove. There's even talk of her running for town council in the next election."

Okay, it was official. I thought I'd returned to Cutter's Cove, but what I'd really done was arrive in some wacky alternate dimension where things were inside out and upside down. "I'm trying to imagine Chelsea as a town council member, but my mind refuses to go there."

"Chelsea isn't the self-centered airhead she was in high school," Trevor insisted. "She's a lot more mature and focused. She seems to care about others and has become a pleasant person since she's been dating Caleb."

"She's dating Caleb?" I asked.

Trevor nodded. "For a while now."

"I guess they did always have a thing for each other," I said. "Or at least Chelsea had a thing for Caleb's money."

"I think their relationship has grown beyond the superficial phase," Trevor offered. "After Caleb came home from New York and Chelsea quit college and took the job at the museum, they started hanging out together. As friends initially. But eventually, they began to date, and while no formal announcements have been made, I wouldn't be surprised if they didn't end up getting hitched."

Wow, Chelsea and Caleb; who would have thought? In high school, he'd been smart, confident, and artistic. She'd been beautiful, polished, and popular, but shallow and self-absorbed as well. Chelsea never paid a bit of attention to Caleb until he found out he was the heir to millions, and then all of a sudden, the boy who'd been an uninteresting geek in her eyes had turned into some sort of a prince on a white stallion.

"So, do we know where Chelsea was on the night Booker was killed?" I asked. I didn't think she'd done it, but I felt compelled to ask.

"According to the notes in the file, Chelsea attended the same party Booker had. When interviewed, she stated she'd been there until the end and had even stayed to help clean up afterward. We know Booker left the party about halfway through and was killed one to three hours after that. It wouldn't be impossible for Chelsea to be the killer if the three-hour estimate is more accurate, but it seems unlikely. I think we're safe in keeping her off any suspect list we might develop, although I think we should speak to her. It didn't appear she knew anything helpful when Woody spoke to her, but we know her better than he does, so we might be able to get something out of her that she wasn't willing to tell him."

"Then let's put her on a list of people to interview who we don't necessarily believe to be suspects," I suggested. "Anyone else?"

"No, that's it."

"When was Chelsea interviewed?" I wondered.

Trev looked at the file. "The day after Booker was killed."

I had to wonder if Chelsea—or anyone else, for that matter—had come up with additional information once they'd had a chance to think things over. I'd have to ask Woody if follow-up interviews had been conducted, although they weren't mentioned in the file, so I assumed they weren't.

Mac, Trevor, and I talked late into the night, so by the time I climbed into bed I was exhausted.

"Wasn't that fun?" Alyson said as she plopped down next to me. She stretched out on her side petting Shadow, who was purring, so I assumed the cat could see her and possibly even feel her touch.

I smiled but didn't answer, hoping if I didn't encourage her, she'd go to sleep. Having ghost me around was like having a puppy: it needed constant attention to be happy.

"Mac and Trevor seemed just the same. Didn't you think so?" Alyson persisted. "They're both so smart and funny. I like the way Mac is styling her hair now. It used to be so wild. And did you notice the muscles Trevor has? I bet he belongs to a gym. Everything feels so right now. Better than it has for a very long time."

I continued to try to ignore her.

"We really do have the best friends." Alyson sighed as she rolled over onto her back.

I had to agree with that. Mac and Trevor were the best friends I'd ever had. They were genuine souls who'd had my back from the moment I'd met them in science class. Now that I was home, I was having a hard time remembering what had kept me away from Cutter's Cove all those years.

"Can we have pancakes for breakfast tomorrow?" Alyson asked, changing the subject.

"Don't you sleep?" I wondered.

"No. You seem to have that covered."

Even though ghost me looked like teenage me, she acted more like five-year-old me. Not that I was that much of a chatterbox even when I was five. I wondered if she was broken. Maybe I needed to have another talk with Chan. "Look, I need to get some sleep, so I'll make you a deal. If you fade away to wherever it is you go when you disappear and let me sleep until I wake up on my own in the morning, we can have pancakes for breakfast."

"Deal." Alyson rolled over and kissed me on the cheek, then disappeared. At least I thought it was a kiss. Her touch didn't put pressure on my skin like a real touch would, but my cheek felt warm where her lips had touched it. I closed my eyes and turned onto my side. Despite what Chan had told me, I was pretty sure I'd completely lost my mind. Still, if I was totally honest with myself, if I had to leave her behind when I went home to New York, I might miss her. It was almost like having an annoying little sister. Something I'd always wanted but never had.

Chapter 5

Wednesday, May 23

I woke early the next morning despite the late night. The sky outside my bedroom window was just beginning to lighten. It looked as if it would be warm and sunny even with the clouds that lingered on the horizon. Shadow stood up next to me and yawned, then dipped into a low stretch before hopping off the bed. I still wasn't quite sure what to make of his presence in the house. Not only had he waited ten long years for my return, but he looked as young and energetic as he had the day I left.

I went over to my closet and pulled a pair of slacks off a hanger. I paused and glanced out the window as the first streaks of red painted the morning sky. I planned to spend much of my day cleaning, so perhaps expensive slacks weren't my best option. I walked across the room to the old dresser I'd left behind and opened a drawer filled with faded jeans.

I picked up the pair on top and held them in my hands. I hadn't worn jeans often since I'd left Cutter's Cove. I rubbed the soft, worn denim over my cheek before slipping them over my long, lean legs. I smiled as I buttoned them over my flat stomach. The jeans felt like a warm hug from an old friend.

I opened yet another drawer and pulled out a light blue T-shirt. Over that I slipped on a white sweatshirt, and then pulled on a pair of Nike's I found in the back of the closet. By the time I made it down to the kitchen, the sky was brilliant with color. The reds mingled with streaks of orange, giving promise to the brilliance of the day ahead.

I made myself a cup of coffee, then wandered out onto the deck. Shadow followed me as I walked along the old beach trail that was now overgrown with weeds. I stood at the top of the bluff, where the trail that wound down the steep cliff began its descent. I listened to the waves crashing onto the sand below as I sipped my coffee and let the peace and serenity of the moment wrap itself around me. The house faced the sea to the southwest, making it ideal for catching sunsets, but during certain times of the year, when the days grow long, the sun rises just over the little bluff on the northeastern side of the cove. The wispy clouds had taken on reds and pinks, indicating that this outing was going to be an exceptionally lovely one.

Memories played gently through my mind as I turned to watch the sun rise over the bluff behind me. I'd first come to Cutter's Cove with a broken spirit and a shattered life, but it hadn't taken long for the easygoing charm of the small town to fill the void left by all that I'd been forced to leave behind. The house had been a godsend. Majestic, yet battered by years of neglect, it had provided Mom and me a project to occupy us. We'd hauled out the garbage and stripped the old, faded wallpaper. We'd torn out the floors and gutted the bathrooms and kitchen. Once the old had been taken away, we began the task of rebuilding. A room at a time. A project at a time. We'd lovingly and carefully added blues, grays, and white, which seemed to bring the feel of the sea into the majestic house. Mom loved to cook, so she'd designed a chef's kitchen. The old hardwood floors had been refinished and every wall had been carefully painted. We'd worked away our grief, our pain. We'd taken something damaged and dilapidated and made it warm and beautiful. With each wall we painted, we'd found peace, and finally, after months of running, we'd realized we'd found a home.

And then I'd met Mac and Trevor, and for the first time in a long time, I'd felt whole. I knew I could never repay them for the friendship they'd shown me, or the impact they'd had on my life, but perhaps I should have tried. I should have called or written. I should have shown them how much they meant to me.

"You're up early," Mac said, sauntering up beside me as I sipped my coffee.

"I wanted to watch the sun rise."

Mac took a sip of her own coffee. "It is something special to watch the sea come to life."

I looked toward the water, which had turned from gray to blue. Seagulls circled overhead, looking for their first meal of the day. "I'd forgotten the feeling of serenity I'd always found here. I can't believe I allowed myself to stay away so long."

"It's easy to let time slip away if you aren't paying attention." Mac put her head on my shoulder. "But you're here now. It's never too late to regain what you've lost along the way."

I took Mac's free hand in my mine and gave it a squeeze. "I'm here now." I closed my eyes and let the feeling float freely through me. "And I intend to make the most of it."

Mac and I stood for several more minutes watching the sun climb into the sky. "How do pancakes sound for breakfast?" I asked.

"Heavenly."

Mac and I went back into the house as the reds and purples coloring the sky gave way to wispy white clouds painted on a blue backdrop. The deep blue sea with white seagulls floating on the surface seemed to mirror the colors of the sky. God, I'd missed this.

When we entered the kitchen, Alyson was sitting at the kitchen table. "It's about time. We're starving."

I frowned at ghost me. I was hungry. Could she feel what I did? I was starting to get used to her presence, but the specifics of whatever was going on was more than a little confusing.

"What's with the frown?" Mac asked as she poured herself a second cup of coffee.

"Nothing. I just ..." I let the sentence dangle.

"I don't think she'll freak out if you tell her about me," Alyson said.

She was right. Mac was the only one who'd known all my secrets. She probably wouldn't freak out if I told her about Alyson. "There's someone in that chair." I pointed to Alyson.

Mac glanced at the table. "Someone? You mean a ghost someone? Barkley?"

"As if." Alyson rolled her eyes. "That old dude has been gone for more than a decade. Ghosts who have moved on don't come back, you know."

I ignored Alyson and shook my head. "No. It's not a ghost. It's me, only it's not me."

Now it was Mac who frowned. "Huh?"

"It's Alyson," I said, giving Alyson a soft look as Shadow jumped into her lap. "Chan said she's the part of me I left behind. The part of me that's connected to the house."

"So, you can see an image of yourself?" Mac asked with a confused expression on her face.

I nodded. "Not just see. Hear and speak to as well."

A look of surprise crossed Mac's face. "Damn. That must have freaked you out the first time you saw her."

I laughed. "Yes. More than just a little bit."

Mac looked at the table again. "What's Alyson doing?"

"Sitting at the table petting Shadow. She's sitting in the same chair as Shadow. Apparently, he can see her. It seems he can even feel her touch."

Mac stood staring at Shadow, her mouth hanging open.

"She wants pancakes," I continued. "It's always been her who loved pancakes."

"Then I guess we should make the pancakes." Mac crossed the room and sat down on the chair next to Shadow. She squinted as she looked at the chair where I'd told her Alyson was. "I wish I could see you. I've missed you. So much. I'm glad you were here waiting."

Alyson put a hand on Mac's leg. A look of shock crossed her face. "She touched me. I felt her touch me," Mac said. "On the leg."

"She did touch you on the leg," I confirmed. "She missed you too."

Mac gulped. "So, is this split permanent? Will you always exist in two different places in time and space?"

I took flour from the cupboard and milk and eggs from the refrigerator. "Chan says we'll be made one again once I'm willing to fully accept Alyson back into my life."

Mac raised a brow. "What does that mean?"

I broke two eggs into a bowl and began to whip them. "Chan says when I left Cutter's Cove to return to my life in New York, I left behind the parts of me that didn't fit. The parts that belong to Alyson but wouldn't fit into Amanda's life. At first, I didn't understand, but I think I'm beginning to."

"And if you're able to reconcile those parts, Amanda and Alyson will merge?"

"Theoretically." I poured the milk into the batter. "The thing is, even if I was able to merge Amanda and Alyson, I think we'll split again when I leave. Alyson is linked to the house." I looked at ghost me, who was twirling her hair as she listened in on our conversation. The thought of driving away and leaving her in the house seemed unimaginable. Yet I needed to go home after I found Booker's killer. Didn't I?

That was much too confusing a question to consider this early in the day, so after I dropped the first of the pancakes on the griddle, I poured myself another cup of coffee and changed the subject. "I thought we'd go to Booker's place today. Talk to Monica. Look around."

"Seems like as good a place as any to start," Mac agreed.

******

Booker's seaside estate was perched on a bluff overlooking the ocean. Built of red brick, the house was a large two-story colonial with single-story wings on either side. The large home was surrounded with magnificent gardens, and the stately interior housed antique furniture and priceless art. Booker had worked as a school librarian, but he'd come from money, and the home he'd created stood as a legacy to the exceptional man who'd loved books as much as Amanda.

"We're here to see Monica," I said to the woman dressed in black who'd opened the door after my knock.

"She's expecting you. Please follow me."

Mac and I followed the maid through the entry, past the grand staircase leading to the second floor, through a large living area with vaulted ceilings and a floor-to-ceiling fireplace, down a hall lined with artwork, and into a room that was even more charming than I remembered.

"Mac; Alyson," Monica screeched.

I was about to correct Monica, but suddenly the distinction between Amanda and Alyson seemed less important.

"It's so good to see you both," Monica said as she hugged us enthusiastically.

"I was so sorry to hear about your uncle," I said.

"He was an exceptional man," Mac added.

Monica's smile faded. "It's been six months, but I still miss him so much. Every time I walk through the front door I expect to find him waiting for me." Monica's eyes filled with tears. "I can't imagine who would have murdered him in his own home."

"I know the police haven't had any luck finding the killer, but Mac, Trevor, and I want to help if we can," I said.

"I spoke to Woody. He said you'd be here to ask me what I knew and to take a look around." Monica looked at me. "I remember you helped to solve mysteries when you lived here. I hope you can help now. It's just not right that Uncle Rory is dead and his killer is still walking around free to do as he or she pleases."

I looked around the large library. It was built on two levels, with the second one open to the first in the center of the room, where a large table and chairs were set. Booker owned thousands of books, collected over a lifetime. It had always amazed me, the depth of knowledge housed in this one room. "I understand he was found in this room."

Monica nodded and walked across the hardwood floor. She paused at a bookshelf on the first floor. "Woody told me it was here."

I glanced at the regal fireplace that had been built into one wall. I could picture Booker sitting in one of the red leather chairs, smoking a pipe. He loved this room most of all in his fabulous house and spent a lot of time here.

I caught a glimpse of Alyson out of the corner of my eye. She walked over to one of the two red leather chairs that faced each other, with a small chess table between them. She sat down, and then poof, Booker was sitting across from her.

I gasped.

"Are you okay?" Monica asked, concern evident on her face.

I glanced at Monica. "Yes. I'm fine. I guess I was just overcome with emotion. Could I possibly bother you for a glass of water?"

"Certainly. I'll bring a pitcher and three glasses. I'll be right back."

Mac gave me an odd look. "What really happened?" she asked after Monica left the room.

"It's Booker. He's here."

Mac looked around the room. "Where?"

I pointed to the red chairs. "There. He's sitting across from Alyson." I walked over to the pair, who seemed to be looking at each other but had yet to speak or attempt to communicate in any way.

"Amanda," Alyson beamed. "Look who's here."

I looked at Booker. "Can you see me? Can you see us?"

"Yes, but why are there two of you? Are you dead too?"

I was surprised to hear Booker's reply; in the past, I'd been able to see ghosts but not converse with them. "No, I'm not dead. This is Alyson. She's the part of me I left behind in Oregon. It's kind of hard to explain. I can't believe I can speak to you." I felt emotion catch in my throat. "How are you?"

Booker looked down at himself. "Dead, so overall, not that great. Are you here to help me move on?"

I nodded. "I think I am. I'm so sorry about what happened."

Booker appeared to frown. "I'm a little fuzzy on that, to be honest. I was at a party. Then, the next thing I remember was waking up to find myself looking down on my own lifeless body. I seem to be stuck here in the library. Every now and then I catch a glance of Monica when she comes in for one reason or another, but I can't touch her or speak to her. In fact, before you showed up here today, I've felt as if I exist in some alternate dimension."

"You don't know what happened? How you died?"

Booker shook his head. "I can't remember."

"Mac and Trevor and I are going to try to find the answers you need. I think we're supposed to be here. I think that's why you can see and speak to me."

"Hey, don't forget about me," Alyson complained.

"Of course," I said. "Alyson wants to help as well."

"Monica is coming back," Mac warned me.

I made a motion, indicating that I needed to stop speaking. I returned my attention to Mac and Monica while Alyson continued to chat with Booker. Apparently, I was the only one who could see or hear either of them, but it was distracting to have them chatting while I tried to ignore them to focus on the living people in the room.

"Let's have a seat at the table and discuss things," Monica suggested. She'd brought both a pitcher of water and one of lemonade and three glasses. "I know it can be hard to take everything in. It took me a long time before I could talk about Booker without breaking down."

Mac and I followed Monica to the table and took seats. It felt wrong to be in this room Booker loved so much without him, but with his ghost just outside my peripheral vision, it was almost right.

"I understand Booker donated this house and the grounds to the historical society," I said to ease into the conversation we needed to have. "I was curious why he might have done that."

"Uncle Rory loved this house and everything in it. He wanted it to be here for a long time. He never married or had children, and his parents, as well as his brother—my father—were dead long before he passed, so the only family he had left were my brother Jessie and me. I know Uncle Rory considered leaving the house to us, but Jessie doesn't appreciate the house the way I do, and I think Uncle Rory was afraid he'd pressure me into selling it. Not that I would have, but I understand why that might have been a concern for him. In the end, I guess he decided it was best to donate the house to the historical society. That way it could never be sold to some random person who might decide to tear it down. He knew I loved the place and would want to live here, so he named me custodian and caretaker."

"I understand you give tours."

"Yes." Monica nodded. "There's a service to take care of the cleaning and the maintenance of the grounds, so the work is easy and leaves me quite a bit of free time. I'm working on a book about Uncle Rory's extraordinary life. He managed to pack in quite a lot during his time on this earth."

I glanced toward the fireplace, where Booker and Alyson were still chatting. He'd been an amazing man and I missed him deeply.

"I know you weren't in town when your uncle died, but I'd be interested in knowing what you've been told," I started off.

"I'd be happy to tell you. If it will help." Monica shifted in her chair. I could sense she wasn't comfortable with this subject. "After Uncle Rory's body was found, someone from the police station called to tell me he was dead. I caught the next flight home. At first, I thought maybe he'd had a heart attack or some other age-related event. He was getting on in years, so his death wasn't exactly unexpected. Then I spoke to Woody, and he told me exactly what had happened. I guess I must have been in shock because the next little bit was sort of a blur. Eventually, I felt able to speak to him about the specifics. I'm glad you're here to help."

I put my hand over Monica's. "I'm glad I'm here too." I looked toward the stacks. "Did Booker ever show you his secret hiding place?"

Monica shook her head.

I got up and walked to the shelf I remembered being the one that held the book that led to the secret drawer. The trick was to pull the book forward and then shove it back right away. A drawer at the bottom of the bookshelf would pop out. It had been ten years since I'd seen the process, but my memory was clear. It was as if I'd watched Booker do it yesterday.

"You remember," Booker's ghost said as I found the correct book and opened the drawer.

I nodded.

"She can't talk to you when Monica's in the room," Alyson said. "Maybe we should just tell her about you."

I wasn't sure that was a good idea. Monica might not take it well, and we needed her to stay calm. I glanced at Alyson, who seemed to understand what I was thinking. She said something to Booker while I retrieved the large envelope that had been left in the secret drawer. Inside was a stack of papers and a thumb drive. I turned to Monica. "Is it all right if we take this with us? I'll have Mac look at the drive and then let you know what we find."

Monica nodded. "Yes. That's fine. I hope whatever Uncle Rory left will help you find the person who killed him."

"Someone killed me?" Booker said. "On purpose?"

Chapter 6

After we left Booker's house Mac and I decided to pay a visit on Caleb. I'd called earlier to let him know I was in town and he'd suggested we meet at the museum so he could show me the changes made since I'd left Cutter's Cove. Caleb and I had met shortly after I'd moved to town, when I was sixteen. Unbeknownst to him at the time, he was the grandson and heir of Barkley Cutter, the ghost I'd encountered shortly after my mother and I moved into his house.

"Alyson, so good to see you." Caleb wrapped me in his arms the moment I walked through the museum door.

"I'm going by Amanda now." I hugged him back.

"Is your mother with you?"

My mom was an artist, the same as Caleb, and the two had become good friends despite the age difference. "No, she's in New York." I looked around the large space filled with relics from the past. "She'd be so excited to see what you've done with this place. The museum was always close to her heart."

Caleb took my hand. "Maybe I'll look her up the next time I'm in New York. I'd love to catch up with her." Caleb pulled on my hand. "Come on. Both of you," he said, as he turned to Mac. "I'll show you what we've done."

The next twenty minutes were filled with a tour of the facility, including the new wing, which hadn't yet officially opened. Caleb had done a wonderful job with the place. Mom was going to be so happy and impressed when I described things to her. As we moved through the building, I kept my eye on Alyson, afraid she'd knock something over in her enthusiasm. Although she didn't have form, so I supposed it wouldn't be possible for her to hit anything even if she did run into it.

Once we finished we went into Caleb's office to talk about Booker.

"I can't believe it's been six months," Caleb said. "I feel his presence here whenever I walk the halls. The museum was such a huge part of him, the items he donated, the work he put into making it perfect."

"Do you have any idea who might have killed him?" I asked.

Caleb shook his head. "I've thought about that quite a lot. But Booker was a kind man who made friends with everyone he met. I can't imagine why anyone would want to kill him. His death isn't just a loss to those of us who were his friends but to the whole community."

"I understand some items donated for the new wing piqued his interest."

Caleb nodded. "It was Illia Powell who donated the boxes of dishes and porcelain pipes. They were obviously very old and I could tell right away that they'd been handcrafted. When Booker saw them, he asked me to wait to display them until he'd had time to do some research into their origin. He suspected they were part of the cargo of the *Santa Isabella*, a ship that disappeared hundreds of years ago. I, of course, agreed, after everything he'd done for us. I still have the boxes locked in a storeroom. I suppose at some point I'll need to set up a display, but I hoped to wait to unveil them after Booker's killer was found. Just in case."

"Just in case the artifacts were related to Booker's death?" I asked.

"Exactly."

"Do you know if Booker made any progress in his research before he was killed?" I asked.

Caleb looked thoughtful. "He told me that he'd found what he believed to be the captain's log of the ship. He felt certain he could use that information to determine where the *Santa Isabella* went down. I pointed out that the boxes were intact and undamaged by the sea, so it was most likely the cargo had been offloaded from the ship before whatever happened to her occurred. He agreed the boxes of dishes and pipes probably hadn't gone down with the ship, but then he told me about the gold buckles he'd found on the beach more than forty years ago. He believed they were part of the *Santa Isabella*'s cargo also. The fact that he'd found them on the beach indicated to him that at least some of the cargo was still on the ship when it sank. I'm not sure he ever reconciled the discrepancy between the idea that the cargo was still on the ship and that it had been offloaded prior to sinking, but I know it intrigued him. I'm sure he'd still be working on it if he hadn't been killed."

"Other than you and Booker, who else knew he was interested in the items?"

"No one except the members of the museum board. I felt it was best to keep them informed about our plans for the donated items every step of the way."

"Did anyone other than Booker seem particularly interested in those items?" I wondered.

"No, not specifically. The entire board was interested to an extent. If Booker could have found proof that the donated items were from the *Santa Isabella*, it would have been a huge find that would have meant a lot of good publicity for the museum. And if he could have found other items from the ship's cargo, that would have garnered national attention."

"Do you think that was what Booker was after? National attention?" I asked.

Caleb shrugged. "I don't know for certain. Booker was pretty tight-lipped about it, and I chose to respect his privacy. He seemed to have a plan, although I wasn't privy to what it might have been."

"Do you think he confided in any of the other board members?"

"Maybe Gilda Joffrey. She was a historian and, like Booker, was interested in how shipping helped carve out the development of this area. They spoke often. My guess is that if Booker did confide in anyone, it would have been her." Caleb glanced at the clock on the wall. "As much as I'm enjoying catching up with you and want to continue this conversation, I have a lunch date with a donor, so I need to run. But let's get together again. Maybe dinner one day this week?"

"I'd like that." I smiled.

"I'll check with Chelsea to see when she's free. She's off today, but I know she'll want to join us." Caleb turned to Mac. "We'd love for you to come as well. And Trevor, of course."

"I'll call you and we can compare calendars," I said.

We left the museum and headed back to the house.

"Despite what Trevor said about Chelsea, I'm having a hard time imagining her with her claws sheathed," Mac said.

I laughed. "Me too. She certainly knew how to rip you a new one without even trying when we were in high school."

"So, what now?" Mac asked.

"I think I'll call Illia Powell. If she's in town, maybe she'd be willing to answer some questions. I don't know that she has any information. Woody's notes made it sound as if she had no idea that the things she donated might have been important. Still, I'd be interested in knowing who she might have told about them. If they were behind Booker's murder, the killer had to have known about them. It sounds as if there were only a handful of people who were privy to that information. I don't necessarily think any of the museum volunteers killed Booker, but maybe it was someone they told about them. Or maybe the leak came from Illia Powell herself."

"Let's call her. If she's in, we'll head there next."

As it turned out, Mrs. Powell was in town to sign papers on the house she'd inherited but had since sold to a family who planned to move in after school let out for the summer. She wasn't due to sign the paperwork until the following day, so she was available to meet with us, answer any questions she could, and even let us have a look around.

The house Mrs. Powell had inherited was a nice two-story structure with a finished attic. Located in the older part of town, where many longtime residents lived, the large yards and shared fences were well maintained, giving the neighborhood a warm, homey feel. While not all that close to the water, it was quaint and charming.

"The house is lovely," I said, noting the rosebushes that lined the front of the blue structure with white trim.

"I've always loved this house," Mrs. Powell said with an expression of longing on her face. "I'd keep it if I could, but my husband has a good job in Seattle and doesn't want to move."

"I suppose you could keep it as a vacation house," I said to the tall, thin brunette.

"I considered the idea, but my husband insists the money we'll receive from the sale will go a long way to allowing us to remodel our primary home. It makes me sad to think the house will no longer be in the family after four generations, but my husband does have a point about the cash." She ran a hand over the top of the white picket fence that lined the lawn. "The family who bought the place are just starting out as a blended family. The couple has two elementary-school-aged children from the husband's first marriage and a two-year-old daughter from the wife's. They're expecting a new baby together in the fall. While I was unsure about selling, the family really seemed to love the house, and I found myself wanting them to have it."

"I'm sure they'll be very happy here," I said.

"How can I help you?" Mrs. Powell asked. "I understand you have some questions about the things I donated to the museum."

"Yes," I verified. "You found the boxes while cleaning out the attic?"

She nodded. "One of the hardest parts about giving up the house, after making the decision to sell it, was the chore of cleaning out four generations' worth of possessions. There were a lot of things purely necessary for everyday use, and just plain junk: old dishes, broken appliances, clothing, and various odds and ends, most of which I donated to a secondhand store. But there was also antique furniture to be priced and sold, as well as several pieces of fairly valuable artwork." Mrs. Powell laughed. "I don't know why I'm bothering you with all this. I know you're here specifically to talk about the items that had been stored in the attic."

"Was everything in it valuable?" Mac asked.

"No. As in the main living space, some of the items were valuable, while others ended up in the dumpster, where they probably should have gone a long time ago. I found a lot of old books, many of them first editions, which I sold to a used bookstore. There were boxes of clothes and children's toys I donated to a church in town. When I saw the things that were stored in wooden boxes with a stamp labeling them from the South American Trading Company, I was intrigued. While I suppose dishes and pipes more than one hundred and fifty years old were an interesting find, I had no use for them, and I decided to see if the museum wanted them. The man I spoke to there seemed excited about getting the boxes, but I've heard since that the donation might be responsible for a man's death. Is that true? Was a man killed over the boxes I found?"

"Honestly, I'm not sure," I answered. "It does appear the things you donated could have led to a man's death, but right now, all we have is speculation. The reason we're here today is to ask you about those items. Do you have any idea where they came from?"

She frowned. "Is that important?"

"It could be," I answered.

She narrowed her gaze. "When I spoke to you on the phone, you said you were working with the police. It occurred to me that if the items I donated were valuable, maybe I should verify that."

I handed Mrs. Powell one of Woody's cards from the small stack he'd left the previous evening. "Call Officer Baker if you like. He can verify that we're who we say we are."

She looked at the card. "I don't think that will be necessary. I don't know anything anyway. It's just that suddenly this conversation struck me as odd."

"That's understandable," I said.

"So, you don't know where the boxes came from?" Mac asked.

Mrs. Powell shook her head. "No, not specifically. I'm sorry I can't help you. There were a lot of things in the attic and I don't know where most of them came from. The boxes I brought to the museum were toward the back, so it seems logical they may have been put up there by one of the first owners of the house."

"Your great-grandfather originally built this place?" I asked.

"He did. Theodore Powell was a fisherman, so I'd imagine items from the sea would have been of the most interest to him. My grandfather didn't inherit his father's passion and went into logging, though that wouldn't preclude him from having acquired the dishes and pipes. Still, it seems more likely it was Great-grandpa who put those boxes in the attic."

"I know you've already cleared out the house, but would you mind if we took a look around?" I asked.

"Sure. Follow me."

The house had been completely emptied. If there ever was anything to find, it was long gone, but we took the tour and thanked her. As we drove away from the old but durable structure, I couldn't help but wonder about all the lives that had played themselves out within those sturdy walls. Four generations; that spoke to me of a permanence I found appealing. The members of my own family tended to move around. The house my grandmother on my mother's side still lived in had been in the family the longest, but even that was only owned by her a bit over thirty years. I was sorry Mrs. Powell had decided to sell the house after all that time, but it sounded like the new family would settle in and make their own new traditions there. The home Mom and I had bought had been owned by four generations of Cutters before us, so it had a long history, even if it wasn't mine.

"It's kind of sad she decided to sell the house," Mac said as we drove toward home.

"I was just thinking the same thing. I love the idea of a home that's loved by each new generation it's handed down to. I love the home Mom and I created together, but it's sort of sad Caleb didn't end up with it."

"You can offer it to him if you ever decide to sell it," Mac said.

"Yes, I guess. It does seem right for Caleb to have it, but I feel connected to it as well."

"Duh," Alyson said. "I think I'm proof the house is meant to be yours."

"I guess you have a point."

"Point?" Mac asked.

"Sorry. Alyson just said that the fact that there's part of me that's literally connected to the house seems to indicate the house and I are meant to be together."

"Alyson is right." Mac whipped her windblown hair out of her eyes. "Do you think you'll ever live in the house again? I mean really live in it, not just visit?"

I was about to say that my life was in New York again before I noticed Alyson's thoughtful expression in the rearview mirror. Was my destiny to end up in the very place I'd found refuge twelve years ago? On the surface it seemed unlikely, but then again…

Chapter 7

Later that afternoon, Mac was working busily on her computer. She'd dropped everything to come to Cutter's Cove to join me, but she still had projects to complete and customers to see to. I decided to use the time to make a list and run to the grocery store. If we were going to be hanging out here in the evenings, I was going to need enough food to feed us. I pulled on a clean pair of shorts and a soft yellow T-shirt, then stared at my reflection in the mirror. All I could see was Alyson. A few days in Cutter's Cove and Amanda seemed to have faded away. I slipped my feet into a pair of sandals and went out to my Mercedes.

"Where are we going?" Alyson asked after I got behind the wheel.

I turned and looked at ghost me, who was sitting happily in the passenger seat. "I thought I'd pick up some food to make dinner."

Alyson grinned. "Nothing Trevor likes better than eating."

I remembered the huge meals my mom used to make for us and smiled. Even at sixteen, Trevor swore he was just a little bit in love with a woman more than twice his age who made a lasagna that could rival even the finest Italian restaurant's.

"You should make Mom's seafood chowder," Alyson suggested. "We could stop by that little fish market on the wharf and pick up some fresh seafood."

"Sounds good." I turned the key in the ignition. "And maybe that little farmers market is open. A nice salad made with locally grown greens would pair with the chowder perfectly." I pulled away from the house and onto the private drive that led to the highway. "And that little local winery used to have a retail outlet not far from the fish market."

"We were too young for wine when we lived here before, but Mom did love their sauvignon blanc," Alyson agreed. "I remember the way her eyes would soften when she sat out on the deck, sipping her wine and watching the sunset. It was hard for her to give up her life and make the move here, but when she looked out over the sea I could see contentment and acceptance on her face."

I remembered. "She did seem happy, despite the situation. And her art; her art was truly inspired here, and so different from the work she'd done before the move."

"Maybe we can talk her into coming out for a few days," Alyson said.

"Maybe." I turned on the radio and settled back to enjoy the drive. It was a warm, sunny day and the urge to shuck all responsibility and drive to the beach was strong. There was something about spring on the Oregon coast that made anyone who was fortunate enough to visit or live there want to break out in song and dance.

"I've really missed this," I said wistfully as I drove along the coast road. "The crashing waves, the rocky shoreline, the white sand beaches, the abundant sunshine."

"So why didn't you visit?" Alyson asked. "The house was waiting. Shadow was waiting. I was waiting."

I rolled down my window and took a deep breath of the salty air. "I don't know. I didn't plan to stay away so long. I guess I just got busy, and the longer I was gone the easier it was to stay gone." I turned slightly to glance at my counterpart. "I can't believe it's been ten years. Now that I'm back, it feels like I never left."

"That's what it's like to go home. No matter how long you've been away, it's always there waiting for you."

I knew for a fact that wasn't always true. After Mom and I were put into witness protection, everyone other than my father was told we were dead. An announcement had been made that we'd died in a car accident, and our family held a funeral for us. At the time, we'd been convinced our disappearance was for the best, but imagine everyone's surprise when, two years later, we'd come home and had to explain we'd always been alive. To say the reintegration into our old lives was awkward was putting it mildly.

When we arrived at the wharf, I found a spot to park near the tall white fence that separated it from the water below. I got out and walked to the little fish market, which, luckily, was still where I'd remembered it. With all the sunshine, there were quite a few people out and about, some fishing, others sharing a meal or beverage at one of the small cafés sprinkled along the boardwalk.

"I see the hot-dog-on-a-stick place is still here," I said as we passed the brightly decorated stand that still hand-dipped the dogs in the batter.

"Oh, and the chili fries." Alyson twirled around in a circle, as if to display her happiness. "Everything smells so wonderful. I'd forgotten."

"I haven't eaten hot dogs or French fries in years."

"Can we have some?" Alyson asked.

"Not today. I want to be sure to save plenty of room for the chowder." I could almost taste the fresh seafood slowly cooked in thick cream sauce with chunks of onion and potato. I continued to the fish counter, where I ordered fresh scallops, crabs, clams, and even a lobster. When everything was wrapped and paid for, I continued down the wharf to the farmers market to buy the greens for the salad. I added a fresh loaf of sourdough bread and a couple of bottles of local wine, then headed back to the car.

"I guess we should get this home," I commented as I put everything on the backseat. "We have what we need for dinner. I think I'll wait and go to the market tomorrow."

"Can we drive down to the beach and put our feet in the sand?" Alyson asked. "Just for a minute?"

I shrugged. "Okay. But just for a minute."

While there were a lot of beaches in the area, the one at the base of the wharf was covered with the finest sand you were likely to find anywhere along the coast. I don't know why the sand in this one area was so different from what was found in other places, but when you stepped into it, the image of silk came to mind.

I found a place to park in the shade and got out of the car. When I got to the sand, I took off my sandals and let my bare feet sink into the softness. It felt heavenly. I walked slowly toward the water's edge while Alyson romped like a puppy. I wondered if this was what it would be like to have a daughter. Ethan and I had never discussed having children. Heck, we'd never discussed marriage. We both lived full lives with demanding jobs. Our undemanding and undefined relationship seemed to suit us. Ethan was sophisticated and ambitious. He loved his high-rise apartment and fast-paced lifestyle. He loved to dine at the finest restaurants and drive the most expensive cars. Ethan was everything Amanda was comfortable with, but I knew he'd find Alyson tiresome.

The sun on my shoulders eased the residual tension I'd been holding on to. The sea was calm and small waves lapped gently onto shore. I felt the chilly water wash over my feet as I stood peacefully and looked out toward the open water. Alluring. Mysterious. Powerful.

I thought about how different my lifestyle was in New York from here as the receding tide pulled the sand from under my feet. I couldn't say I was any happier here than I was there, or vice versa. It was as if I were two different people living two equally awesome but very different lives.

On a whim, I pulled out my cell and called Ethan. I'd meant to be in touch every day I was away, but somehow the hours seemed to fade one into the next and I hadn't called since I'd arrived in Cutter's Cove.

"How's the investigation going?" Ethan jumped right in, before I had a chance to say hello.

"We're only just getting started."

"Any chance you'll be cutting your trip short? I have tickets to the June Regatta. Personally, I find it tiresome, but you know how important these things are to my career."

I paused. "The regatta is in just two and a half weeks."

"That's right. June 9."

"I really don't think I'll be back that soon. I've only just arrived."

Ethan didn't respond right away. I could picture his face as he chose his words. Ethan was an exacting man who rarely spoke before he'd given himself time to think. "I know you've only just arrived, but I hoped that once you got there you'd realize Carson Cove is no longer part of your life."

"Cutter's Cove," I corrected. "The town is called Cutter's Cove."

"Yes. Well, whatever. The point is, you no longer live there. Your life is in New York."

"I know. And I do miss you. But honestly, being back has been wonderful. I've only just begun to get the house in order, but it already feels like home. If you were here, you'd understand. Maybe you can fly out for a weekend? I'd love to show you the house and introduce you to my friends."

"You know how busy I am."

"Yes." I sighed. "I know."

"Please give the regatta some thought. If I want to get that promotion we both know I deserve, I need to be seen at the right events."

I bowed my head and looked at my feet as the water rushed over them, splashing up onto my shins. "I know, I really should go. I just wanted to say hi, but I have seafood in the car for the chowder I'm making for dinner."

"You're cooking?" Ethan sounded as shocked as if I'd told him I planned to perform brain surgery.

"Yes. I like to cook."

"We've been dating for two years and I've never seen you cook a single thing. In fact, I'm pretty sure the oven in your apartment still has the new appliance packaging inside."

I had to laugh at that. "It very well might, and you're correct, I don't cook in New York. Cooking is more of an Alyson thing than an Amanda thing. Amanda likes to dine out and Alyson likes to cook."

Ethan paused again. Longer. His silence seemed to speak volumes. "Should I be worried about this whole dual personality thing?"

I glanced at Alyson, who was chasing seagulls along the surf line. "Not at all. Having to live as two different people can be confusing, but I've missed being Alyson. I'm enjoying spending time as her again. I really do have to go. I'll call you tomorrow. And go ahead and give the second ticket to the regatta to someone else. I won't be back for at least a month."

I hung up and turned back toward the car. I guess I didn't blame Ethan for not understanding why I would want to return to a life that had been forced upon me by a very tragic set of circumstances. If I'd never left New York, I'm very certain Amanda Parker would never have wanted to visit a small coastal town on the opposite side of the country. Becoming Alyson wasn't something I'd wanted at the time, but now that she was a part of me, I treasured it very much.

Driving along the coast road with the wind blowing through the open windows made me wish for the first time I'd bought a convertible rather than a sedan. Of course, a convertible in New York was completely ridiculous, but a convertible on the Oregon coast would be just about perfect.

"Stop," Alyson screamed.

I slammed on my breaks, which caused my tires to screech and my backend to fishtail as I came to a stop.

"What is it?" I asked as my heart pounded with adrenaline.

"There's a dog."

I looked around. It hadn't felt as if I'd hit anything. "Where?"

"There." Alyson pointed to a shallow ravine on the side of the road.

By the time I'd pulled the car over to the shoulder and parked, Alyson was already gone. I got out of my car and walked to the edge of the drop-off. At the bottom of the ditch, a few yards back from where I'd stopped, was a lump of gray with Alyson standing over it. I carefully made my way toward where she was crouching. Laying on his side was the most pathetic-looking dog I had ever seen.

I bent down for a closer look. "Hey there, pal," I said softly.

The dog peered up at me with sad eyes. He wasn't bleeding, so I didn't think she'd been hit by a car, although there was no way to know for sure.

"She's scared," Alyson said.

"Yes," I agreed as I slowly ran my hands over the matted fur, checking for injuries. "She's so thin. Her ribs are sticking out and she smells bad." I held my breath and turned my head away. "Really bad."

"Maybe a skunk?"

"Probably."

"We need to help her," Alyson said.

I looked back toward the car. I cringed as I considered putting this stinky, filthy dog in my new Mercedes. "Okay." I carefully lifted the dog, which looked to be a lab or retriever mix, into my arms. She whimpered and trembled but didn't snap or struggle. I walked as carefully as I could to my car, opened the back door, and slipped her inside. I was conflicted as to what to do with her now that I had her. A trip to the vet was a must. Just before I closed the door the dog whimpered and looked back at me with thankful eyes. I went around to my trunk and grabbed a bottle of water from the stash I always traveled with. I found an empty travel mug and returned to the dog's side. Carefully pouring water into the mug, I offered the dog a drink. It was a messy method of delivering water and more of it ended up on my seat than inside the dog, but eventually, she stopped panting and laid her head down. I closed the door once again, got behind the wheel, and headed back down the highway.

When we arrived at the same veterinarian's office where I'd taken Tucker, I went inside and explained my dilemma. I didn't have an appointment and the dog wasn't bleeding or outwardly injured, so I had no reason to believe an emergency appointment was necessary, but the receptionist was a kind woman who insisted I bring her in so she could have the vet take a look. I opened the door and slipped on the leash and collar she lent me. The poor dog began to tremble as I lifted her out of the car.

"It's okay," I whispered as I set her gently on the ground. I was glad to see she was able to stand and support her own weight. "I know doctors are scary, but I'll be with you the whole time."

"Me too," Alyson piped up.

The dog seemed uncertain, but she obediently followed me into the waiting area, which, thankfully, was empty.

"That's a powerful smell," the veterinary technician said as the dog nervously shoved her face into my lap.

"She must have gotten into something," I apologized as I slowly stroked the dog's head.

The woman's eyes softened. "Let's get her on the scale."

I got up and led the dog down the short hallway. When we arrived at the scale, which was only a few inches off the ground, I bent down so I was eye to eye with her. "We need to weigh you. Can you climb up?" I patted a hand on the scale. The dog slowly stepped onto it.

"Sixty-two pounds. She should be at least ten pounds heavier. I'm sure the doctor will give you some food designed to put the weight back on."

"Thank you," I said to the woman, who led me into a small room with an aluminum table. There was nowhere to sit, so I simply crouched down and petted the filthy dog, trying to ignore the stink while I spoke softly to her. After less than two minutes, a woman in a white lab coat walked in.

"Isn't Dr. Jones here anymore?" I asked. The woman who had treated Tucker had been older, with short gray hair. This woman was young with long blond hair pulled into a braid.

"She retired two years ago. I'm Dr. Roberts. Tina Roberts."

"Nice to meet you." I shook her hand.

"I'm going to run a few tests to check for anything that might require immediate attention, but if those come out okay, I'm going to have you take her home, give her a bath, feed her with the high-protein food I'm going to give you, and ask you to bring her back in a few days." The vet looked in her ear. "I'll give you drops for her ears and some vitamins as well."

"I imagine she's a stray," I said. "We should check to see if someone's looking for her, though."

"I'll check with the nearby shelters and put a notice on my website. Once she's cleaned up, take a photo of her and send it to me. I'll post it on my bulletin board." The vet paused. "Given her condition, I'm going to guess no one's looking for her. Still, you never know what the poor thing has been through."

I looked at the dog, who was visibly shaking. Poor thing. My heart bled for her.

An hour later, I left with one bag of calorie-dense dog food and another with medicated shampoo, pills, drops, and instructions. My plans to spend the afternoon cooking were suddenly down the drain. I just hoped the seafood I'd purchased would still be okay to cook the following day. Tonight looked like we were in for more pizza.

"Oh my, who's this?" Mac asked when we got home.

"A stray Alyson found on the side of the road," I explained as the dog limped suspiciously toward Mac, who had bent down to greet her.

"She seems like a sweetie, but she desperately needs a bath."

I held up the bottle of medicated shampoo. "A bath will be my first order of business once I get the food I bought put away."

"You go on ahead with the bath and I'll take care of the food," Mac offered.

I smiled. "Thanks. Call Trevor and have him bring a pizza. I realize that will be pizza two nights in a row, but I won't have time to make the chowder by the time I get this girl cleaned up."

"I'll call him. I like pizza. And Trevor won't mind."

Luckily, the dog cooperated when I got her into the bathroom. I decided a shower would be easier, so I adjusted the water temperature until it was just right, stepped in, shorts and all, pulled her in, and closed the shower door behind us. The poor thing was terrified at first, so I slowly ran the handheld shower head over her body to wet her fur, speaking slowly and gently the entire time. The shaking lessened, and she began to relax. I imagined the warm water felt good.

"If you aren't used to a shower, this may be frightening," I said in a soft voice, which I hoped the dog would find soothing. "I bet that warm water is nice." I ran my long fingers along the dog's back, working out some of the knots in her fur as I did so. "Your coat is a beautiful shade under all that grime," I commented. I could feel the dog begin to relax as I slowly massaged the shampoo in. I squatted down to make sure I wasn't getting any soap in the dog's eyes. She reached out and licked me on the cheek. "You're welcome," I said as I began to rinse the first lathering of shampoo out of her fur.

I shampooed her twice more and rinsed her thoroughly. I grabbed a large, thick bath sheet to dry her as best I could before opening the shower door. Even after having been towel dried, her fur held a lot of moisture, so when she shook, water went everywhere. I'd have to add *clean bathroom* to my list of chores.

After her bath, I took her downstairs and into the kitchen. I measured and poured the amount of food the vet had recommended into one of Tucker's old bowls that we'd left behind. I filled a dish with water as well and then left the dog to eat while I went down to the basement room we'd used for storage to look for Tucker's old dog bed.

We'd left so much behind. Most of the things from our lives here, in fact. Mom and I both knew the things that belonged to this life would have no place in the one we were returning to.

"She looks and smells a lot better," Mac said when I returned to the kitchen.

The dog was curled up on the rug in front of the brick fireplace. Alyson sat on the floor stroking her while she napped. I glanced at the bowls of food and water. Both were empty.

"There was a really good conditioner in the shampoo. I managed to work most of the mats out, but there are a few that will need to be trimmed. I'll do it when she wakes up." I looked at the dog bed I'd lugged up from the basement. "I'll just put this in my room and then I'll be back down." I looked out the window. "It looks like it's going to be a breathtaking sunset. I bought wine if you want to open it and head out to the deck."

"Sounds perfect."

When I arrived on the deck, Mac was sitting in a lounge chair, a glass of white wine on the little table next to her. Beside that was a second glass of wine, and on the other side of the table another lounge chair. I noticed there was a third chair nearby, for Trevor when he arrived.

Mac had pulled the large kitchen rug out onto the deck. The dog and Alyson were both curled up on it, and both appeared to be sleeping, although I remembered Alyson didn't sleep, so perhaps she was just resting. Either way, she looked completely happy. I wondered when the last time I had been as content was. Probably the last time I sat on this deck and watched the sun set with someone I cared about as much as I cared about Mac.

I sat down in the chair, which was arranged to face the ocean. The sun was just beginning its descent. It was going to be a beautiful sunset, just as I'd imagined. "Did you get hold of Trevor?"

"I did. He'll be here at eight with pizza. Is Woody coming?"

"No. He called me earlier and said he wasn't able to reschedule his prior commitment. I'll fill him in tomorrow." I leaned back in the chair, taking a sip of my wine as the warmth of the setting sun warmed my face. The sea was calm, and the air barely moved with a gentle breeze. It was odd, but in some ways, I felt as if I'd suddenly woken from a dream and found myself home.

"What are you going to name her?" Mac asked.

"Name her?" I turned my head slightly.

"The dog. You're going to keep her, aren't you?"

I frowned. "I can't keep her. I'll be going home in a few weeks."

"They don't allow dogs in New York?"

"Of course they do, but I live in an apartment and I have a job that keeps me away from it for most of the hours of every day." I took a sip of the wine. "That's why Tucker lives with my mom. She has a house and a yard and is home most of the time."

"If you aren't going to keep her, what are you going to do with her?"

"I don't know. I haven't had a chance to think about it. I guess I'll keep her here for a week or so in case someone's out there looking for her. If I don't find her people, I guess I'll ask the new vet to find her a home."

Mac didn't answer, but there was a very doubtful look on her face. I knew what that meant.

"I'm not keeping her," I insisted.

"Uh-huh; we'll see."

"It's not an option."

Mac raised a brow before taking a sip of her wine.

I looked at the dog curled up so peacefully with Alyson. Suddenly, I knew this was exactly what it would be like to have a child. My heart warmed at the thought before I chased it away.

"The dog should have a name even if she's only with us for a short time," Mac insisted.

"How about Skunk? The inside of my car smells so bad, I'm seriously considering burning it and getting a new one."

"I suppose you could do that. If you really wanted to."

I hesitated. "I wasn't really going to burn the darn thing."

"I know. But if you wanted to, you could afford to buy a new car without missing a beat."

I shrugged. "I guess. I told you Amanda came from money. Old money and a lot of it."

"You did tell me that, but somehow it never fit with what I knew of Alyson. I guess this is the first time I've considered what you had to walk away from."

I turned away. Suddenly, the conversation had become a lot more serious than I'd intended. The sky began to turn orange as the sun dipped toward the horizon. I glanced at the dog, whose gray coat was now a soft reddish gold. "How about Sunset?" I said. I looked at Mac. "For the dog. We can call her Sunny."

Mac smiled. "I like it."

Sunny thumped her tail even though she didn't bother to lift her head.

"I think she likes her new name," Mac said.

"Yeah. I think she does at that."

Chapter 8

As promised, Trevor arrived at eight o'clock with a six pack of beer and a pizza. Mac and I both elected to stick with wine, so he popped the top on his beer can and joined us at the dining table, where I'd set out plates and utensils as well as a large green salad to go with the pie. It felt welcoming, homey, dining on the cobalt-blue dishes my mother had picked out when we'd lived here together. The dishes were a perfect contrast to the rich color in the cherrywood table, which went nicely with the pale gray walls framed with white crown molding. The house had been such a mess when we first moved in, but after a lot of time, love, and elbow grease, we'd managed to accomplish our goal of bringing the feeling of the sea and the sky indoors.

Sunny was awake after her nap. She greeted Trevor but seemed content to watch us eat from the nearby rug. Mac had mentioned the dog to Trevor on the phone, so when he stopped for the beer, he'd picked up a ball, a chew toy, and a stuffed doggy for

Sunny to play with. She seemed to appreciate all her gifts but had curled up with her stuffed puppy with such care and nurturing that it almost seemed as if she thought it was a real animal. I wondered if she'd had pups at some point. I'd ask the vet when we went in for our follow-up.

"I bet she's going to be a beauty once you brush her out," Trevor said.

"Her coat is an exceptionally rich color. I don't suppose you're in the market for a dog?" I asked.

Trevor raised a brow. "You found her. According to the rules of nature, that makes her your dog."

"Maybe, but I'm only here for a few more weeks. I can't keep her for the long run."

Trevor took a bite of his pizza. "I see."

I see? What did that mean? I wanted to ask, but I didn't want to put a damper on the peacefulness of the evening, so I changed the subject. "I was thinking it would be fun to go surfing while I'm here." I looked at Trevor. "It's been a decade, so I imagine I suck, but it's still something I'd like to try. Do you ever have a day off? A whole day?"

"Pirates Pizza is closed on Mondays. We could go then. Spend the day at the beach. Bring food to grill and maybe build a bonfire when the sun goes down."

"I'd absolutely love that." I turned to Mac. "Are you in?"

"Absolutely. We'll go to a beach that allows dogs so Sunny can come."

I grinned as Sunny thumped her tail without looking up from her comfy position. It seemed as if she already knew her name, which wasn't likely, though she seemed to respond to it.

"I was going to wait to bring up the murder until we were finished eating, but I wanted to remember to tell you that I ran into Walter Brown today," Trevor informed us. "He came in for lunch."

I remembered Walter Brown was the retired doctor Woody had spoken to, a volunteer at the museum and a friend of Booker's. "Did he have anything to add to the notes Woody had in his file?" I asked.

"He told me that Woody interviewed him the day after Booker's body was found. At the time, he couldn't imagine who would kill such a nice, generous man, but he's had time to think about things and he's come up with a very loosely developed idea."

"And what would that be?" I asked.

Trevor took a bite of his pizza before he answered. He chewed slowly, swallowed, and washed it down with a sip of his beer. "Walter told me that Booker had confided in him about some health issues he'd been dealing with in the months before his death. It seems he had a very minor heart attack about eight months before he was murdered, which caused him to take a realistic look at himself. Walter thinks that was about the time he spoke to Caleb about the donation to the museum."

"That makes sense. I'm sure when you get to be Booker's age, you think about your own mortality quite a bit," I said. "I don't know his exact age, but I imagine he was in his late seventies or early eighties."

"Seems right," Trevor agreed. "Anyway, Walter said it was after his heart attack that Booker seemed to change his approach to certain things. He became a lot more careful about what he ate and drank, as well as the amount and intensity of the exercise he got, but he also seemed to become a bit more reckless."

"Reckless?" I asked.

"Walter said Booker wanted to leave behind a legacy. And not just the donation of a new wing to the museum or the house to the historical society; he wanted to do something important, noteworthy. He thinks Booker realized he didn't have a lot of years left, and he decided to jump into the pool of life and grab on to as many different experiences as he could, hoping one would lead to the type of legacy he had in mind."

"Booker was already the type to look for life experiences," Mac pointed out. "He'd traveled the world and done more than most by the time we'd met him."

Trevor nodded. "True. But the life experiences he sought earlier in his life were exactly that—experiences. Walter felt Booker wanted to put his name on some sort of academic or artistic endeavor. He wanted to create something or discover something. He wanted his name to come up in conversation years after he was no longer with us."

"So, he wanted to do something like prove that the cargo from the *Santa Isabella* ended up right here in Cutter's Cove," Mac said.

Trevor shrugged. "Walter didn't know about Booker's theory about the cargo, so he didn't mention that specifically, but he did indicate that he was looking to do something just like it."

"Let's take a minute to deconstruct this," I said. "Several things seemed to have occurred at around the same time. First Booker suffered a minor heart attack that put him in touch with his mortality, or at least we assume that's what occurred, and then at just the moment when he was looking for something that would put him on the map, so to speak, he found out that items had been donated to the museum that seemed to confirm his theory that the *Santa Isabella* sank in the water off Cutter's Cove, not farther south, as most assumed. It makes sense that he might decide to take hold of this clue he felt he'd been provided and run with it by looking farther into the idea that the missing cargo was right here in Cutter's Cove."

"Makes sense," Trevor replied. "The question is, how did he plan to go about proving his theory and possibly even finding the cargo?"

"I wonder if he found something else," I mused. "Something more that would have pointed him in a direction."

"Mac, you said you planned to look at the stuff you guys found in Booker's secret drawer this afternoon. Did you find anything interesting?" Trevor asked.

"I did, although I didn't stumble onto anything to suggest where the cargo might be or what Booker hoped to prove by searching for it. Hang on; I'll get my notes and catch you up on what I know."

"It looks like everyone is done with the pizza," I said to Trevor. "Let's clean this up and move the discussion into the living room."

Trevor began stacking the bright blue plates one atop the other. "I can't believe how much you've gotten done in just a few days."

"I spent some time dusting the downstairs and ran the vacuum around. The windows need washing, but I thought I'd hire someone for that, and I haven't even touched the upstairs other than my bedroom and the guest room Mac took."

Trevor went into the kitchen. "I know a guy who can do the windows and any other heavy work you want to hire out. His name is Vern. He's a good guy. Hard worker. And he doesn't charge an arm and a leg. Or I guess you could talk to Sam Sutton about having Carter Carson do it. Might give you a chance to chat with him about his time at Booker's."

"That's a good idea. I'll call Sam tomorrow."

Trevor grabbed a pad and a pen that were on the counter from earlier in the day. "I have the number. I have Carter do things for me at the restaurant when Vern isn't available."

I stuck the number on the refrigerator so I wouldn't forget to call the following morning. Trevor and I returned to the living area just as Mac looked up from her computer. We settled onto the overstuffed furniture and waited for her to begin.

Mac settled back into a large comfy chair, stacking a pile of papers on the ottoman in front of her. "First off," she began, "the papers we found in the envelope were mostly photocopies of documents. There were a few copies of pages from old books as well. I haven't had time to look at them closely, but it appears everything in the file is a copy of something old. Very old."

"We can go through them tomorrow when we have more time," I suggested.

"That's what I figured as well. I hoped to have time to work on them today, but I had a few things to do for work and I wanted to focus on finding out what I could about the items on the thumb drive."

"And what did you find on that?" I asked.

"Not a lot. The drive contains files. Some, such as ships' manifests, are easy to access; others are secured with passcodes. I'm sure I can get into the protected files without too much trouble, but it could take time with the limited equipment I have here, and I didn't have time to work on them today. I have some work to do tomorrow for my employer, but I should have more time to commit to our project than I did today."

"Nothing really jumped out?" I asked.

Mac looked up. "I didn't say that. I did find one thing that could explain a lot. One very big thing."

"Okay," I said. "You have my attention."

"As we've already discovered, the *Santa Isabella* was a cargo ship that dealt mostly with perishables such as silk, tobacco, and slaves, as well as handcrafted items such as pottery, glassware, and pipes. While the cargo of transport ships had value, they usually didn't take on gold and precious jewels so as not to attract pirates. I found something in Booker's notes in his secret hiding place. It seems he saw an entry in the log he found stating that the captain of the *Santa Isabella* had agreed to take on twelve trunks of gold coins. The coins aren't listed anywhere on the manifest. Only in the captain's log."

"So, the captain was moving the gold under the radar," I said.

"That appears to be the case."

"And while old dishes and pipes don't seem to be valuable enough to kill a man over, a dozen trunks of gold coins certainly would be," Trevor said.

"Exactly. I'm unclear, however, whether Booker shared the information about the gold with anyone. So far, no one has mentioned it to us. I'm also unsure whether the log Booker found really belonged to the *Santa Isabella*. Booker seemed to think it did, and he was a very intelligent, educated man, but it seems odd to me that the log would just be sitting in a used bookstore, where it seems he found it. The ship sank more than a century and a half ago. Where has it been all this time?"

"Good question," I acknowledged.

"Booker was a brilliant man, but he was also a dreamer. It seems the chance of his finding gold buckles from the *Santa Isabella* on the beach near Cutter's Cove forty years ago, and then a captain's log from the same ship in a used bookstore, only to be followed by boxes of cargo from the same ship in the weeks before he died, is pretty unlikely."

"So how can we find out if the log is legitimate?" I asked.

"I don't know," Mac admitted. "I think we should proceed as if something is there but keep in the back of our minds that Booker's death may not be related to the ship or its cargo at all."

"Maybe we should ask him about it," I suggested.

"*Ask him* about it?" Trevor asked.

"When we went to Booker's house today, he was there. In the library," I said gently.

"What do you mean, he was *there*?" Trevor asked.

"His ghost was there. Monica was in the library for all but a few minutes, so I couldn't have a long discussion with him, but he didn't remember his death. He remembered the events leading up to it, though, and then he remembered floating over his body."

"That must be so weird," Trevor said.

"I imagine it is. I'd like to have a longer chat with his ghost. He should be able to tell us if he told anyone about the gold coins. Real or not, they could serve as a motive for getting him out of the way. I'm hoping if we can speak to him, he'll be able to help us narrow things down. But I'm not sure if I should tell Monica about my ability to see ghosts and her uncle's presence in the house, or if I should try to get in and talk to Booker alone when she isn't there." I looked at Trevor. "She was the one who introduced us to him. How do you think she'd react to being told there's a ghost in the house where she now lives?"

Trevor paused before answering. "I'm not sure. I didn't know her all that well in high school, and she moved away after we graduated. She only came back after Booker was killed, and I've only run into her a few times since. I remember her as being pretty open-minded, but I can't say for sure how she'd react to living with her uncle's ghost."

"Maybe we should arrange for you to speak to Booker alone, Amanda," Mac suggested. "He might have an opinion on Monica's reaction."

"I guess we can come up with a reason to go back to the library. You can come up with a reason to get Monica out of the room, can't you, Mac? Maybe ask her to show you something, or use the I-need-a-drink thing again. Hopefully, Booker will be there and I can talk with him while you're gone."

Alyson, who had disappeared when we'd moved to the living room, suddenly reappeared. "Alyson has joined us," I informed the others.

"Alyson has joined us?" Trevor asked with a look of confusion on his face.

I looked at him sheepishly. "Oh, I guess I haven't filled you in." I quickly explained about Alyson and my split personality. I could tell that Trevor was surprised and somewhat confused, but he was a trooper so he didn't question my sanity as most would have. He simply made a few jokes about always wishing there were two of him and moved on. I returned the conversation back to Booker's murder as quickly and smoothly as possible.

"You spoke to him for a lot longer than I did today," I said to Alyson. "Did he say anything we should know about?"

Alyson sat down on an empty chair. "Mostly we just talked about what it was like not to have form. When you told Booker he'd been murdered, he was both shocked and irate. He never imagined he hadn't died of natural causes. If you ask me, he'd be as determined to find his killer as you are."

"Good. We can use that."

"How about a little help here?" Mac said.

I told Mac and Trevor what Alyson and I had just said. It certainly would be easier if they could see her as I did. Better yet, it would be best if I could somehow figure out how to get her back on the inside. I wondered, though, if her being on the outside was the reason I could speak to and understand Booker today.

Mac and I went up to our rooms after Trevor left. It had been a long day and I was exhausted. Sunny followed me upstairs, waiting patiently at the bathroom door while I brushed my teeth. Then I showed her the dog bed I'd brought up for her. She sniffed at it, then jumped up onto my bed.

"Oh no," I said as she put her head on my pillow. "Dogs don't sleep on the bed." She lifted her head slightly, looking at me with soulful eyes. I couldn't believe she'd even been able to make the jump, considering she could barely walk earlier in the day. I was about to lay down the law about the bed when Alyson appeared. She snuggled up next to the dog, who began thumping her tail on the mattress.

"The dog sleeps on the floor," I said with what I hoped was a tone of authority.

"Come on, Amanda. She's clean, and you have a big bed. Let her stay."

Alyson draped an arm over the dog's neck. Sunny laid her head back down on the pillow and closed her eyes. Shadow appeared from the hallway and jumped up to join them. Apparently, the matter was settled and I had absolutely no say in it. I considered physically moving the dog to the floor, but it might be nice to sleep with a dog again after all these years. I changed into my pajamas, turned off the light, then took the empty side of the bed. The window was open slightly, bringing the sound of the waves into the room. I slowed my breathing and focused on the steady rhythm as I drifted off to sleep.

Chapter 9

Thursday, May 24

The sky was still dark when I woke up the next morning, but I could sense the first rays of dawn just over the horizon. Sunny was still asleep on the bed, but Alyson and Shadow were gone. I slipped out from beneath the covers and pulled on a pair of baggy sweats and my high school sweatshirt. Blue and gray. I smiled at the word *Pirates* splashed across the front. Had it really been ten years since I'd worn this while sitting on the sidelines of the football field, rooting for our team? Blue and gray. The colors of the house, the sea, and my past.

In the bathroom, I washed up, pulled my hair back from my face, and then returned to the bedroom. Sunny looked up, lifted her head, and thumped her tail in greeting. She looked better today. I found an old baseball cap, put it on my head, and then softly called her to follow. I made a pot of coffee before pulling on the Nike's I'd left in the mudroom and took the dog out for her morning walk.

Out of old habit, I headed toward the bluff. That was where I'd always headed. That vantage point framed the waking sea as the sky turned from dark to brilliant. When I got to the edge, I paused. I'd spent a lot of early mornings standing on this very spot, watching the world awaken, while Tucker ran around and did his business. I felt a tug at my heart. I placed a hand over my chest and remembered. Tucker hadn't lived with me for quite some time, and to be honest, after a first few days of sadness, I hadn't minded. I'd been busy, and Mom had the time for him. But now, standing in the exact place where I'd spent so many mornings with the funny, playful puppy who'd quickly grown into a large and protective dog, I missed him. He'd been my companion. He'd never questioned, only loved. He'd stood by me through everything I'd endured. He'd been my rock. He'd saved my life.

I took a deep breath and forced the memories to the back of my mind. Longing for what once was wasn't a productive way to spend the first hours of a new day. While Alyson enjoyed a laid-back, easygoing way of life as a teenager, Amanda had a career. No time for pointless thoughts that no longer had a place in her life.

I pulled the phone from my pocket and looked at the time. Mom was an early riser and it was three hours later on the East Coast, so I decided to call. Even if she hadn't yet started her day, she wouldn't mind. She never minded.

"Amanda. I'm so glad you called," Mom answered after the first ring. "I was just thinking about you. I've wondered how things are going. How you're settling in."

"I'm good," I said as the first glow of red shone on the horizon. "Really good. We haven't found Booker's killer yet, although it's early in the investigation. Mac and I are settled into the house. It's really been wonderful being here." I turned to gaze at the large structure that felt more like home than anywhere else I'd ever lived. "Trevor comes over every evening, just like he used to." I looked back at the first blush of color in the sky. "He misses your cooking."

"And I miss cooking for him. I never met anyone who enjoyed a meal as much as he did."

"And still does," I added. "It almost feels like the past ten years never happened. In some ways, it's like I've stepped back in time. Except for the fact that you and Tucker aren't here. I miss you." I paused for a heartbeat. "I miss you both so much."

I heard rustling in the background, as if Mom was changing position. "I didn't think I missed the house or our life by the sea," she said after she'd settled. "Not really. Not once we were home. But now...Now that you're there, the memories have been flooding back." I heard Mom's voice catch just a bit. "We were happy there."

I smiled at Sunny, who wandered over with a stick in her mouth. I bent and took it from her. "We were."

I tossed the stick and Sunny barked.

"Is that a dog I hear?" Mom asked.

"A stray Alyson and I found yesterday."

"*Alyson and I?*"

"Yeah. I guess I should explain," I said, and then I did. In the beginning, I'd hidden my ability to see ghosts from my mother. I hadn't thought she'd understand. I wasn't sure *I* understood. But after a while I could see her mind had begun to open to all the possibilities our life by the sea provided. When I'd shared my visions with her, she'd been surprised but not shocked. Having a daughter with a split personality, though, was another thing entirely.

"Wow. I don't know what to say."

"It came as quite a shock to me as well. At first, I was pretty irritated by her, but she's starting to grow on me."

"You speak of her as if she's a totally different person," Mom said softly.

"I guess I do think of her that way. Sort of like a little sister who has my memories and can taste the pancakes I eat. The whole thing is very odd. But…"

"But?"

"I don't know. I guess if I leave Cutter's Cove— *when* I leave—I think it's going to be hard to leave her behind."

"She can't come to New York with you?"

"Not according to Chan," I said, reminding Mom who he was. "She's the part of me that's attached to the house. But she's more than that. She's funny, and impulsive, and, quite frankly, very immature for someone our age. Chan said she's the part of me I intentionally left behind, that I knew wouldn't fit in Amanda's world." I watched the sky grow lighter as the gray turned to color. "I guess I understand that. Even when I was here, and all my parts were whole, I lived a life that would never have fit into the world we did before. The world we went back to."

Mom didn't respond, her silence spanning several breaths. "Did we make a mistake?"

"I don't know," I said. I inhaled and pulled myself together. "What's done is done and all we can do is go on from here." Sunny put a paw on my knee, as if reminding me that I still needed to throw the stick she'd brought back. "Anyway, back to Sunny. Alyson spotted the dog while we drove down the highway yesterday. I didn't see her at first, but Alyson screamed for me to stop. I pulled over, and that's when I saw her in the ditch. Gray, fragile, and stinky as hell."

Mom laughed. "I can imagine. Do you remember when Tucker took on that skunk that lived under our house?"

"I do, and that's exactly how Sunny smelled. Anyway, she appears to be on her own and has some medical issues. She has pills to take. Special food. Drops for her ears. I know I can't keep her, but I figured she could stay with me for the time being. Until her owner is found."

"And if it isn't?"

I glanced at the dog, who seemed to have double the energy she had the day before as she returned once again with the stick. It looked like having regular feedings and healing pills were already working. Today, I'd brush out her matted fur. "I guess I'll cross that bridge when I come to it. There's a beautiful sunrise today," I added, mentioning the reds and oranges and the calm sea.

"I did love those sunrises." Mom sighed. "And the sunsets."

"You should come to visit while I'm here. Your old room is waiting just the way you left it. It would be fun to spend some time together in a place only you and I can truly appreciate."

Mom hesitated. I was sure the idea appealed to her. "I have that gallery showing next week."

"So come after that. I plan to be here for at least a month. Possibly longer."

"I hate to leave Tucker. He has pills to take and exercises to do every day."

"Bring him. Call Cubby to see if he has time to fly you out. Both of you." Cubby was a friend who owned his own small jet. He ran charters and usually made time to take me wherever I needed to go. I'd thought about asking him to fly me out when I came west, but the urge to drive had been overwhelming.

Mom took several breaths. "Are you sure?"

"Very sure. Mac and Trevor would love to see you, and as odd as this is going to sound, I know Alyson misses you. Please. It would make this trip even more perfect than it's already been."

"Okay." Now Mom sounded hopeful. "If Cubby can bring Tucker and me, I'll come out for a few days after the show. I'd love to paint a few more sunsets to add to my collection, and I've been missing that kitchen."

I grinned. "The kitchen is great. Still as perfect as when you designed it. And your studio in the attic is just waiting for your return. I can't wait for you to get here. Come as soon as you can. You can paint while Mac and I try to solve Booker's murder. Trevor owns Pirates Pizza now, so he's busy during the day."

"Trevor owns the pizza parlor?" Mom sounded as surprised as I'd been when I'd first found out.

"He's all grown up. I mean, he's still Trev, but he has his own business and a nice apartment. Or at least he told me it's nice. I haven't been there yet. It does seem he's done well for himself. And Mac too. She works for some big tech firm and makes a whole lot of money."

"I think you all did well for yourselves," Mom said.

I paused as the first rays of sunshine peeked over the mountain, wrapping me in their brilliance. I hugged my arms around myself. "I guess we did at that."

After I hung up, Sunny and I went back to the house. Mac was sitting on the deck, so I poured myself a second cup of coffee and joined her. "It's going to be a warm day."

Mac nodded. "I'm so enjoying your view. It truly is spectacular. If I lived here I don't think I'd ever get any work done."

I took a sip of my coffee. "The view is quite spectacular, but you do get used to it. When I lived here, I always enjoyed it when I took the time to sit out here, but it didn't distract me to the point that I couldn't get anything else done. You said you had work to do today?"

"Unfortunately, yes. I took off in a hurry when Trev called, and I have projects to complete and customers to take care of. I think I may just bring my computer out here."

"That's a good idea. There are electrical sockets near the big table in the corner." I stretched out my legs, letting my feet rest on the railing. "I spoke to my mother. She says hi."

"How is she?"

"Good. She has a gallery show next week, but she might try to come out for a visit after that."

Mac smiled. "I'd love to see her. I noticed she left some of her work upstairs."

"We just took a few things when we left. I guess we both intended to come back."

"But you didn't."

"No."

Mac leaned her head back, letting the sun hit her face. She looked peaceful and contented. Sunny had headed for the laundry room, where I'd left her food and water when we'd returned from our walk, but she must have finished because I noticed her standing at the slider. I got up and opened the door for her and she found a spot in the shade and drifted off for a nap. I wondered where Alyson was. I hadn't seen her all morning.

"I think I'll run to the market this morning," I said after a while. "We could use a few things. Milk. Eggs. A loaf of bread. I'll start a list. Let me know if you have items to add."

"Maybe some yogurt. Are you going back to try to speak to Booker today?"

I nodded. "I'd like to, if I can figure out how to work around Monica."

"If you wait until this afternoon, I can go with you. I'll figure out a way to get Monica out of the library while you talk to Booker. Unless he has a real problem with us filling Monica in on his presence, I really do think it would be easier to tell her what we know."

"Yes," I agreed. "I'll speak to Booker and we can figure things out from there."

******

By the time I got to the market the day had turned hot. I wore a pair of white shorts and a colorful blouse with a geometric design. Opting for my old flip-flops over the low-heeled sandals I'd brought from New York, I felt cool and comfortable and very much like Alyson, who still hadn't appeared before I left for town, which was beginning to worry me.

I'd decided not to keep the seafood from yesterday. It was probably all right, but after I'd taken Sunny to the vet and returned home it had been sitting in the car for quite a while. Better safe than sorry. I considered replacing the things I'd purchased and making the chowder tonight, but considering the abundance of sunshine the morning had brought, I elected to buy some steaks to grill. I had the bread I'd purchased the day before along with the rest of the greens I'd found at the farmers market. A few heads of corn to grill with the steaks and we'd have the perfect springtime meal.

I'd just rounded the corner toward the bakery when I heard someone call my name. My old name.

"Is that Alyson Prescott?" Chelsea Green chirped.

I turned and smiled. Dark hair. Green eyes. Porcelain skin. "Chelsea. How are you?"

"I'm wonderful." She closed the space between us and gave me a genuine hug. "I heard you were in town. It's so good to see you."

"It's good to see you too. Trevor tells me that you and Caleb are dating."

Chelsea's whole face lit up. "Crazy, right? When we dated in high school I'd pretty much figured we were too different to really make a go of things, but here we are ten years later and very much in love."

"Congratulations. I'm happy for both of you."

"How about you? Married? Engaged?"

"Neither," I answered. "I do have a boyfriend. Ethan. He's an attorney back in New York."

Chelsea put her hand on my arm. "That's wonderful. And you? Are you an attorney too?"

I shook my head. "I'm a graphic designer for an advertising agency. I won't go so far as to say it's my dream job, but it's fast paced and competitive, which I like, and the pay is fine."

"That's so funny. I always pegged you as the type to go into law enforcement. You seemed to like getting tangled up in all those mysteries you, Mac, and Trevor used to spend your time investigating. I never saw you as the artsy type."

Chelsea had a point. I wasn't sure how I ended up where I had. I supposed I drifted from one opportunity to the next until I landed, and I'd probably inherited my interest in art from Mom. "I hear you work at the museum. You worked with Booker before he was murdered."

Chelsea's lips tightened, and anger flashed in her eyes. "Booker was a good man. A hardworking, honorable man. He didn't deserve to die the way he did."

"Do you think his death had anything to do with the donation the museum received? I understand he was quite intrigued by it."

"I kind of doubt it. I mean, why would anyone kill over a bunch of dishes? I understand why the museum might consider the stuff a windfall, but I can't see how it could be worth someone's life. Caleb seemed to think there was something more. Something Booker wasn't telling us, so maybe…"

I waited for Chelsea to continue, but she didn't, so I changed the subject. "And how do you like working at the museum?"

Chelsea shrugged. "I like it okay. It brought Caleb and me together, and for that I'll always be grateful. I'm not sure I have the same appreciation for dusty old boxes scavenged from local attics as some of the others, but it's a good job for now." Chelsea looked at her watch. "I have to go, but I'd love to catch up when I have more time. Give me your number and I'll call you."

I rattled off my digits and Chelsea punched them into her phone before she turned to go. Then she stopped and said, "Listen, if you and the others decide to look in to Booker's death, which I just realized is probably the reason you're here, you might want to speak to Oliver Pendergrass. He bought the marina south of town a few years ago, and I know he has a salvage ship he rents out from time to time. Booker mentioned in passing that he had a theory about where some cargo might have ended up, given where the ship went down and the drift and tides. I don't see how anyone can figure something like that out, but he seemed confident he had a location worth searching. I overheard him saying he'd hired Oliver to take him out for a look. In fact, I'm pretty sure they went more than once. It seemed they got along just fine. But then, the week before Booker was murdered, I heard them arguing."

"About what?"

"I'm not entirely sure. I'd stayed late at the museum and Booker came in with Oliver. They headed to the little office Booker had and closed the door. I didn't want to interrupt, but before I left I heard Oliver say he was getting what was due him come hell or high water. He sounded really mad."

"Did you tell this to Woody?"

Chelsea nodded. "He spoke to Oliver, who claimed they were arguing about a poker game. He swore what I overheard was just good-natured ribbing. I don't think Woody believed him, but he didn't have any proof he was lying, and I didn't hear anything specific enough to pin his anger on any business deal they could have been engaged in." Chelsea put both hands on her basket, as if to push away. "I can't say with any certainty that Oliver was responsible for Booker's death, but if you ask me, he sounded mad enough to kill."

Chapter 10

When I returned home with the groceries, I was relieved to see Alyson playing with Sunny on the front lawn. Or what was left of the lawn. After ten years of neglect, it was more of a weed patch, but it was green and offered a contrast to the sandy soil.

"Where have you been?" I asked her after I'd pulled up in front of the house and exited the vehicle.

Alyson looked confused. "I don't know. How long was I gone?"

I took a couple of bags from the trunk. "I'm not sure exactly. You were in the room with me when I fell asleep last night but gone when I woke up this morning." I turned toward the front door with the groceries in my arms. "When you fade away, do you go to a place? A physical place? Or are you just suspended in some sort of limbo?"

Alyson shrugged. "I never thought about it. I remember being in bed with you and then being on the lawn with Sunny and Shadow." Alyson glanced toward the front porch, where Shadow was lounging on the front porch swing. "I don't know where I was in between or how long I was there."

I climbed the steps to the front porch, opened the front door, and walked inside. Mac saw me come in and went out to the car to grab a couple more bags while I went on into the kitchen. "It must be odd to just pop in and out the way you do. Can you control it?"

"I think so. I know that since you've been here all I have to do is want to be somewhere and there I am. I'm sorry if you were worried about me. I'll try not to fade away for so long."

I set the groceries on the counter and began emptying the bags.

"What are we going to do today?" Alyson asked.

I opened the refrigerator and began loading up the crisper. "I want to go back to Booker's house to try to talk to him again. I didn't have a lot of time to question him about his memories of the night he died. I'm hoping he'll be able to fill in some of the blanks. After that, I hope to arrange interviews with some museum volunteers. Oh, I ran into Chelsea at the grocery store."

"I wonder if she ever found her footing."

I paused and looked at Alyson. "Found her footing?"

"She had a tough time when we were in high school. She never felt like she fit in or had any real friends."

I raised a brow. "She was the most popular girl in school. Head cheerleader. Homecoming queen. Every boy's fantasy. As well as pushy and obnoxious."

"Fake. Nothing was real. She tried so hard, but it never felt right to her."

Alyson could be right. I'd sometimes seen a look of loneliness and longing in her eyes. "I think she found herself along the way," I said. "When I saw her today, she seemed happy. Settled."

"Did you remember the ice cream?" Alyson asked, peering into one of the bags.

Talk about a short attention span.

"Three kinds. If you want to come with me to Booker's, stick around. I'm going to go over as soon as I get these groceries put away and I'm not going to wait if you aren't around."

"I'm not going anywhere," Alyson assured me as she sat on the counter. "If you want to get Monica out of the room, bring something to share that she'll have to serve. Like cake or pie. We can talk to Booker while she fetches the plates and utensils."

"That," I smiled, "is a very good idea."

"What's a good idea?" Mac asked as she walked in with a load of groceries.

"Alyson suggested we bring something for Monica to share. A cake or pie that she'll want to serve. I can chat with Booker, providing he shows, while Monica gets the plates and flatware."

Mac set the bags on the counter. "That *is* a good idea." She looked around the room. "I wish I could see Alyson."

Alyson wandered over and took Mac's hand in hers. Mac smiled. "She's here, isn't she? Holding my hand. I can feel her."

I nodded. "She's holding your hand. You know, maybe if you practice, you'll eventually be able to see her too. I think the fact that you can feel her is really something."

Mac's phone rang, breaking the spell. Alyson walked away while Mac looked at the caller ID. "I need to take this."

She walked out onto the deck and I continued to put away groceries. I'd ended up buying enough to feed an army. I hoped Trevor would keep coming by so everything got eaten.

"That was work," Mac said a few minutes later. "I'm afraid I have to log in and help a customer who's having problems with an update. I wanted to go with you to Booker's, but it looks like this could take most of the afternoon."

"No problem," I said. "I'll take Alyson and we'll stop to buy a cake to distract Monica for a few minutes. I should be home in a couple of hours. I bought a ton of food, so help yourself to whatever. Oh, and if Trev calls, let him know we're barbecuing so he doesn't stop for food on his way over."

After making sure all the groceries were where they belonged, I headed to the door. Sunny followed me, hoping to come along, but I wasn't sure Monica would want her in Booker's house. "Sorry, sweetie, you can't come this time. We'll take a walk when I get back."

Sunny whined and stretched out on the floor and stared at me with her huge sad eyes. Darn it; I hated to leave her when she looked at me like that. Sad eyes were exactly the reason I'd sent Tucker to live with Mom. In New York my life had become so full. I'd hated leaving him home day after day, even when I hired a dog walker. Eventually, I'd admitted he'd be better off with Mom.

Alyson bent down and whispered something in Sunny's ear. She stood up, wagged her tail, and headed up the stairs.

"What did you tell her?" I asked as I went out the front door.

"I told her that I hid a treat for her under your bed."

"And did you?"

"Of course. I wouldn't tease. Shotgun," she called as she appeared in my front seat.

******

I'd called ahead to let Monica know I planned to stop by. I'd said I needed to reference a few of Booker's books to understand how his project to find the *Santa Isabella* might play into his death. Really, I had no idea what sort of information I might be looking for, but Booker had loads of books on the history of shipping on the Oregon coast; I figured asking to check out his books was as good an excuse as any to spend some time in the library.

As Alyson had suggested, I'd brought a treat to share. I'd been thinking cake but ended up with brownies.

"Alyson, I'm so glad you stopped by," Monica, wearing a cute yellow sundress, greeted me.

"It's Amanda now."

"Of course. I'm sorry. It's hard to get used to the change."

"Not a problem." I handed Monica the bag. "I brought brownies."

"I love brownies." Monica smiled.

"A cup of coffee to go with them would be perfect," I hinted.

"I'll make some. Go on back to the library. I'll bring everything when the coffee's ready."

Bingo. Just as I'd planned. I headed down the hallway with Alyson skipping behind me. I was glad no one else could see her. If she were solid and humanlike and appeared to everyone, I wasn't sure how I could explain a teenager who looked exactly like me but acted a lot more immature than I had ever been even as a teen.

"Booker, are you here?" I said aloud as I walked into the library and closed the door behind me.

He appeared just a few feet from where I stood. "I sent Monica to get coffee, so we need to talk fast. I'm of the opinion you have knowledge that could help us catch your killer, but it would be easier if we could speak freely. How do you feel about telling Monica that you're here?"

Booker didn't answer right away, though he appeared to be giving my question some thought. Eventually, he said, "I agree it would be easier if she knew I was here, but I don't want to scare her. I'm not sure how she'd feel about living in a house with a ghost she can't see."

"I can see she would always be wondering if you were lurking. Watching."

"I seem to be trapped in the library, so I suppose that would ease her mind on that count." Booker paused and then continued. "Perhaps you can work the subject of ghosts casually into the conversation and see how she reacts."

"Okay. Before she comes back, though, I want to ask, do you have any theories at all as to who might have killed you?"

"I've thought of little else since you were here. I'm not sure this lead will pan out, but I hired a man to help me look for the cargo."

"Oliver Pendergrass?"

"Yes. How did you know?"

"Chelsea told me about him. Do you think he killed you?"

Booker shook his head. "No. But I think he could have told someone about the cargo I was looking for, and that someone might have decided to look for it on their own."

I rolled my lips one against the other to moisten them. "Who do you think he told?"

"I don't know. But the house was broken into while I was away a week or so before I died. The alarm sounded, and the police arrived after only five minutes, so whoever broke in didn't have a lot of time in here. It appeared at first that nothing had been taken, and the police assumed the alarm had scared the intruder away, but later, after they left, I found that two of the books that had been on my desk were missing."

"Books about the *Santa Isabella*?"

Booker nodded. "The only two books I had dedicated to ships during that time period."

I took a deep breath. "Okay. That's unfortunate, but it does give us an avenue to investigate. Chelsea said you and Oliver had an argument in the days before your death. She was in the museum when the two of you came in. She left shortly after, so she didn't hear much, but from what she did hear, it sounded like Oliver was pretty angry."

"He was. I accused him of flapping his lips and spreading the news that I'd hired him to find the cargo from the *Santa Isabella*. He denied it, but I didn't believe him. I told him I had no intention of working with a man who couldn't keep to the confidentiality agreement I'd had him sign and was inclined to look elsewhere for a ship, and he yelled back at me that one way or another, he was getting what was due him."

"So you promised him something for finding the treasure or cargo or whatever it was you were looking for."

Booker nodded. "I'd been paying him a small daily fee with the promise of a large payout once I find what I was looking for. I could see why he was mad. If I fired him, he would lose the payout. On the other hand, if he was blabbing…"

"I think at this point…" I stopped talking abruptly when I heard the tea trolley roll up to the library door. Monica opened it and rolled the trolley inside.

"Here we are. Coffee with brownies, as requested."

"Thank you so much. I feel like such a pest, asking you for coffee you didn't have already made, but I got up early and have been running around all day. I really needed a chocolate and caffeine pick-me-up."

"It wasn't a problem at all," Monica said. "I'm just grateful you've come all this way to help find Uncle Rory's killer. I know how busy you must be in New York. The fact that you remembered Uncle Rory and want to help means a lot. Anything at all you need, just ask."

I smiled as I watched Booker and Alyson go over to the chairs in front of the fire where they'd sat the previous day. Did ghosts need to sit? I couldn't imagine that gravity affected them, so they shouldn't need to take the weight off their feet.

"When we researched the ship we were looking for back when we first met, Booker had a couple of books relating to shipping in this area. Old books. Books yellowed with age. I was sure I remembered where he'd shelved them, but I don't see them now."

Monica's lips tightened. "Woody told me that Uncle Rory reported a theft the week before he was murdered. Someone took two of his books. Two of his old books. I seem to remember they were related to the history of shipping in this area. If you can remember the names of the books you're looking for, you can check with Woody. I'm sure my uncle gave him the specifics."

I sat down at the table and took a sip of the coffee Monica had brought. It was good; I took another sip. "I'll check with Woody, but chances are they're the ones I was thinking of." I lifted a brownie from the larger plate and transferred it to one of the two small ones Monica had brought with her. "It seems the cargo your uncle was looking for may have been the motive for his death, although I won't go so far as to say I'm discounting other possibilities. I think focusing too tightly at this point would be a mistake."

"I agree in theory, but who?"

"I spoke to Chelsea Green today. She mentioned a man named Oliver Pendergrass."

Monica nodded. "I know of him. His name was brought up before. I'm pretty sure Woody cleared him, but perhaps you should ask him to fill you in on what he found." A tear lingered at the corner of Monica's eye. "I've tried to participate in the investigation to the extent I've been asked, but it's so hard. I can't imagine what Uncle Rory went through in his last minutes. It horrifies me to even consider it, so I've tried to block out the details and let the professionals do what they're paid to do."

I put my hand on Monica's. "I totally understand."

"My brother doesn't understand why I agreed to move into this house. He's angry Uncle Rory didn't leave it to us, and he doesn't understand why I would want to help when in his eyes, we've been slighted. But I really do see why Uncle Rory did it, and I like living here. I feel close to him when I'm in the house or walking through the gardens he spent so much time tending. This may sound strange, but I can feel his presence in this house. Especially in this room."

"It doesn't sound strange at all. And I'm sure he is here. Watching over you."

Monica smiled sadly.

"I don't know if I ever told you this, but when I first moved to Cutter's Cove, I saw a ghost."

Monica looked doubtful. "A real ghost?"

I nodded. "It was Barkley Cutter. I'd never seen a ghost before, but from the moment I moved into the house where he had lived and died, I could sense him. I felt his presence for days, watching me, judging me, waiting to make his presence known at just the right time. When he did appear, I wasn't surprised to see him. Some part of me knew that once I'd accepted his presence he'd come to me."

"How did he look?"

"His features were faint, like a blurry watercolor. Otherwise, he looked like he had in life, gnarled and wrinkled, his back curved with age. Yet he was translucent and airy. Like gossamer suspended in space."

Monica leaned forward. "Were you scared?"

I shook my head. "I knew he wouldn't hurt me. He came to me because he needed my help. He's the reason I became involved in my first investigation. Since then, I've seen other ghosts. Some, like Barkley, needed my help; others just appeared as if to say hello, or maybe to check me out."

"Can you see Uncle Rory? Is he here in this house?"

I glanced at Booker, who had his attention on our conversation. I decided to take a chance. "He is here."

"Where?" Monica looked around, turning her head in as close to a full circle as one could.

I pointed. "There. By the fireplace."

Chapter 11

Monica got up and walked across the room, tears streaming down her face. "Uncle Rory. Are you here? Can you hear me?"

She stopped walking. Booker touched her arm. A look of surprise crossed her face. "I can feel him. On my arm. It felt warm, as if a hand touched me."

"He did touch your arm. He hopes you aren't too freaked out by his presence. He wants me to assure you that he spends all his time in the library and isn't lurking around in the rest of the house."

Monica frowned. "I'm not freaked out, but if he's here, that means he hasn't moved on."

"He seems to be trapped here for the time being. I'm hoping if we can find his killer, he'll be free to move on to the afterlife. That's what happened with Barkley and a few of the other ghosts I encountered."

Monica reached out a hand, as if to feel for him. She slowly pulled her hand back and then returned to the table where I was still sitting. "We need to help him. We need to find his killer."

"We will," I said with a certainty I was far from feeling. "We will," I said again, as if to convince myself.

"Where do we start? What do we do?" she asked.

"I'm going to ask Booker some questions. It will seem odd to you because you'll only be able to hear my side of the conversation, but I'll explain when I'm done."

Monica looked scared, but she nodded.

I turned back to Booker. "Woody told me that on the night you died, you'd been to a party. Several people who were there told him that about halfway through the evening, you received a text and left. It was your housekeeper who found your body the next day, but the medical examiner put time of death at one to three hours after you left the party. Do you remember where you went?"

Booker paused, as if trying to pull up the memory. "I'm not sure. It's all a blur. I remember the party. Chelsea and Caleb were there. I spoke to them, as well as a few others. I remember leaving early, but I can't remember why."

"You left after you received a text. Try to remember who it was from."

Booker faded out but faded back in after a few seconds. "I do remember the text. It was from a man named Dredge. Or at least I think it was."

"Dredge?"

"I'd forgotten it until this minute. After I learned that others were aware of my project and suspected Oliver had broken the confidentiality agreement I'd insisted on, I looked around for someone who had a ship comparable to his. It was very important to me that whoever I hired understood the importance of secrecy. I asked around at the marina and was given the name of a man who preferred to operate off the radar. That was fine with me. That was what I was looking for."

"This man arranged to text you on the night of the party?" I asked.

Booker nodded. "I let my contact at the marina know I was interested in speaking to this man about a job. A couple of days later, my contact brought me a cell phone and told me that Dredge would text me to set up a meeting. I didn't know when he would be in touch, so I carried the phone with me all the time."

"Why all the cloak-and-dagger stuff?" I wondered.

"I'd been warned Dredge wasn't always selective in the jobs he signed on for. It seems he was equally likely to salvage illegal items from the sea floor as legal ones. I guess that required him to be very careful."

"Illegal items?"

"Drugs. Stolen goods. He operated up and down the coast, from Alaska to South America. Really, wherever the money took him."

"And you didn't mind the fact that he dealt in illegal salvage?"

Booker paused. "That did give me pause at first, but I was on a timeline and my source assured me that not only was he willing to take on new work for the right price, but he was good at what he did. He had the equipment I needed and seemed the sort to keep his mouth shut, so I agreed to meet him."

"On the night you died?" I asked. "You met him on the night you died?"

Booker frowned. "I'm not sure. It's a little blurry, but maybe." Booker scratched his head, or I suppose it would be more accurate to say he scratched at where his head would have been if he had form. "What I do remember is that I accepted the phone as well as the terms, and then I waited."

"What terms?" I asked.

"Dredge wanted a lot more money than Oliver had asked for, and he required a hefty deposit. The amount gave me pause, but in the end, I decided I didn't care about the money. I just wanted to find the cargo and prove once and for all that my theory about where the *Santa Isabella* sank was accurate."

"Try to remember receiving the text during the party. Several witnesses said you received one, so I'm going to assume that's exactly what occurred. Woody said he found your personal cell, and the text wasn't sent to it. That makes sense based on what you've just told me about Dredge."

"I guess it does make sense." Booker got up and began floating around the room, what seemed to be the ghost equivalent of pacing. "I wish I could remember."

"Try to relax. Picture yourself at the party. See the room. See the people you spoke to. Remember what you ate and what you drank. Remember what you were wearing."

Booker stopped floating and sat back down in the chair. He looked uncertain, and I waited. The answer to who'd killed Booker was trapped somewhere in his memory.

"The party was an evening affair," Booker began. "I wore my blue suit, but I'd lost quite a bit of weight since I had my heart attack, so it hung loosely on my body. I had a belt to cinch up the pants, but I remember asking Chelsea if she knew a tailor she could recommend. She jotted down a few names, which I put in my shirt pocket. We chatted for a bit after that, but then Caleb waved to her, so we said good-bye. I was going to head out for a breath of air when the phone in my pocket vibrated. I took it out and looked at it. There was a time and place in the text." Booker smiled and looked up. "I remember. It said Rinaldo's at nine p.m."

"Rinaldo's the restaurant? The one north of the commercial fishing marina?"

Booker nodded. "It burned down about five or six years ago. The shell is still standing, but so far, no one has gone to the effort of tearing it down and rebuilding on the land. I said my good-byes and went out to my car." He paused, as if pulling at a thread he couldn't quite unravel.

"And then what? You went out to your car and what?" I asked.

Booker began floating around again. It appeared he was focusing intently on my question. "I somehow knew I was to come alone. I guess that might have been part of the terms I'd previously agreed to. I was supposed to bring the fifty-thousand-dollar deposit. The money was in the trunk of my car. I'd kept it close once I agreed to the terms so I'd have it on hand if an agreement was reached."

I lifted a brow. "Sounds dangerous to agree to meet a man you've never met in a deserted location after dark carrying fifty thousand dollars."

"Yes. Considering what happened, it wasn't a very good idea."

Poor Booker. I was sure remembering must be hard on him, but his memories were our best bet at finding out what had happened the night he died. "Okay, you went to Rinaldo's. You went alone with the fifty grand. Then what happened?"

Booker paused once again. He faded out and then back in. I could see the effort to remember was taxing for him.

"It's okay," I encouraged him. "Take your time and let it come to you."

Booker nodded. He settled back in his chair. Alyson reached out and took his hand in hers. He began to speak again. "I remember pulling up in front of the burned-out building. It was dark. Really dark. The closest street lamp had been damaged. Maybe during the fire. I walked up to the building with the money in my briefcase but was unsure what to do. I was thinking it probably wasn't safe to go into the building. It had been condemned. Someone came up from behind me."

"Dredge?" I asked.

Booker slowly shook his head. "I don't think so. Maybe one of his men. He was a big guy. He patted me down and took the phone I'd been texted on, as well as the money in the briefcase. He asked if I had any proof of the general location where the ship went down. I told him I had a copy of the captain's log I'd discovered years ago. There were notes that provided clues, and from those notes, I felt I had enough to map out a search area."

"The man you met wanted to be sure you weren't chasing windmills."

Booker nodded. "It seemed he didn't want to waste his time on a salvage operation with no basis in fact. I suppose I didn't blame him."

"And the captain's log? Did it outline where the ship had sunk?"

Booker tilted his head to one side. "Sort of. I probably didn't have the kind of proof this man wanted, but in my own mind I'd learned quite a lot. The log told me that the captain took on some gold coins. A lot of them. He didn't include them on the ship's manifest and most of the crew didn't know about them. It seemed the captain was promised a percentage of the value of the coins if he smuggled them to Russian-occupied southern Alaska."

I glanced at Monica. She was intent on my half of the conversation, but I had to hand it to her; she hadn't interrupted once to ask what Booker was saying. She demonstrated a lot more patience than I would have had our roles been reversed.

"Okay. The captain was smuggling gold coins on his own ship. I'm assuming he needed to get the coins where he was going without putting into port in San Francisco. How did he accomplish that?"

"I'm not completely sure, but I seem to remember he hijacked his own ship. He must have brought a few others in on what he was doing. All I know for certain is that he continued north rather than putting into port in San Francisco. There was a struggle. Maybe the others who weren't part of the plan revolted. Based on the description of what occurred, it sounded as if the ship hit a reef during the struggle and began to take on water. Based on the captain's notes on the coastline, I'm certain the ship sank not all that far off the coast, just south of Cutter's Cove. The lifeboats were loaded with the men and as much of the cargo as could be transported. Whatever wasn't loaded into them went down with the ship."

"So, the items that were donated to the museum must have come ashore on the lifeboats, and the gold buckles you found washed up on the beach all those years later must have gone down with the ship."

"That would be my best guess," Booker confirmed.

"And the gold?" I asked. "Surely someone would have grabbed the gold before they did the crates filled with dishes and porcelain pipes."

"It would seem they would have, but I'm not sure. As far as I know, the gold hasn't been found. I thought I'd find the wreck, and if the gold wasn't there, I'd look to see if it was buried on shore."

I paused and briefly explained to Monica what her uncle had said so far.

"Something feels wrong," Monica said when I finished catching her up.

I frowned. "I agree. Why would the crew grab dishes and pipes and leave the gold belt buckles, even if they didn't know about the gold coins?"

"Maybe the boxes were labeled and someone switched things around," Monica suggested. "During the chaos as the ship began to sink, the crew must have grabbed the boxes labeled *gold belt buckles* without taking the time to look inside."

"Maybe. I guess at this point the details aren't important. What's important is figuring out how all this relates to your uncle's death." I turned my attention back to Booker. "Okay, so you told the man you met that you had the captain's log and then what?"

"He wanted to see the log. I was pretty sure he worked for Dredge, but he wasn't the man I'd hired. At any rate, I didn't have the captain's log with me, but I said I could get it. I didn't want to take him here because I didn't trust him, so I arranged to meet him again the following evening. Same time, same place. I insisted that Dredge himself be there. I never received confirmation of that, however."

"And then?" I asked.

"And then I left."

"And the fifty thousand dollars?"

"He gave it back to me and told me to return with it when I had the proof Dredge needed to take on the job."

I caught Monica up again.

"It sounds like this Dredge was a legitimate businessman, even if he did deal in illegal as well as legal bounty. He gave Uncle Rory his money back until he provided the proof he needed, and he certainly didn't have to. I don't imagine Uncle Rory had a gun and physically, I'm sure the intermediary had the upper hand."

I looked back at Booker. "After the money was returned to you…what did you do then?"

"I came home."

"And once you got here?" I prodded.

Booker's memory was returning, but it seemed to come in spurts. There was no way to know if there were holes in the story, but any amount of information would help. "I don't remember driving home, but I remember being in the library. I was dressed for bed, so I must have let myself into the house, changed into my pajamas and robe, and poured myself a brandy. I must have built a fire because I remember there being one. I was sitting at the table going over my maps and charts. I remember taking a sip of my brandy and then pausing when I heard a noise."

"And then?" We were getting close. If only he could remember what happened next.

Booker shrugged. "And then I was floating over my body."

"Where were you at the last moment you can remember being alive?" I asked.

"In the library."

"Where specifically in the library? Were you standing? Sitting? Near the fire or near the bookshelves?"

"I was sitting at the table. Is that important?"

"Maybe. Woody told me that you were found over by the stacks. You must have gotten up to get a book. Maybe the intruder asked you to get it, or maybe he wanted information you had in your secret drawer."

"No one knew about that except you, Mac, and Trevor. Not even Monica."

"Maybe the intruder was after a book he thought you might have on the shelf. The captain's log?"

Booker scowled. "The log was in my wall safe. Is it still there?"

I looked around the room. "Where?"

"Behind the painting of the ship on the far wall."

I crossed the room and pulled away the painting. Booker gave me the combination and I opened the safe. The log was the only item inside.

"Was there anything else in the safe?" I asked out of curiosity.

Booker's eyes grew big. "The fifty grand. I remember now. I put it in the safe when I got home."

Okay, that seemed important. "So, someone broke into your home and demanded that you open the safe. You did. They demanded the fifty grand but left the captain's log right where it was. Seems like the intruder was after cash, not necessarily the treasure."

"Those gold coins, if found, are going to be worth a whole lot more than fifty thousand dollars," Booker said.

"True. But maybe the intruder didn't know about the gold. Maybe he was only after the cash. Do you always leave cash in your house?"

Booker shrugged. "Occasionally."

"What cash?" Monica interrupted for the first time.

I paused to catch her up.

"So, we have no idea if the person who killed Uncle Rory was after the cargo he hoped to find or if his death was the result of a home invasion gone bad?"

"It would seem." I paused to look toward where Alyson was waiting. She hadn't made a peep or interrupted in any way. "I think I'm going to have another chat with Woody. Maybe if we put our heads together, we can come up with something. Mac is looking into some things as well. If you'd like, you can join us at my place tonight. We're having dinner while we discuss the investigation."

"Thank you," Monica said. "I'd like that."

I turned back to Booker. "I can see that this has been hard on you. I'm not going to push you any more right now. I'll come back tomorrow. Try to remember who came in. The person who caused the sound that seems to be the last thing you remember is most likely the person who killed you."

Chapter 12

I headed to Woody's office from Booker's. I felt it was significant that the money Booker had in his safe had been taken, while the captain's log had been left behind. Maybe Oliver Pendergrass had found out Booker was talking to Dredge and decided to take the money he felt was owed him. Or maybe Dredge decided to take the easy fifty grand after all, rather than messing around with the larger but harder-to-get-his-hands-on treasure. I wondered who else might have known about the money.

"Alyson, I'm glad you stopped by," Woody greeted me.

"It's Amanda. Did you find something?"

Woody picked up a file. "Let's go back to the conference room."

I followed him down the narrow hallway. This place really could use a facelift. Yellowed walls, which I suspected had at one time been white, were lined with narrow doorways leading to small rooms, each featuring dirty gray linoleum that had probably been there for decades.

At least the conference room was a bit larger than some of the other rooms. It was windowless, with a long table and ten plastic chairs. I sat down on one of them, wondering what Woody had to say that was interesting enough that he wanted to speak without the threat of being overheard.

"Do you have news?" I asked again, eager to get on with it.

"I do." Woody turned slightly and pulled a laptop that was sitting on the opposite end of the table. "I'm not sure it's important or significant, but it's new nonetheless."

"Go on."

"It occurred to me after we spoke that Ms. Parish had already been in the house cleaning for several hours before she found Mr. Oswald in the library. I wondered if she'd been asked about evidence she may have cleaned up prior to finding the body. She told me that no one asked her about it, but there was sand in the foyer when she came in. The first thing she did was sweep it up and then run a mop over the tiles. She said the foyer was clean when she left the day before, so it's possible Mr. Oswald tracked in the sand, but she thought he would have swept it up had he done so."

"I agree. Booker was very neat. If he tracked in sand, he would have cleaned it up. My guess is that the killer did it. Did the housekeeper notice anything specific about the sand?"

"She said it was unusually fine. Most of the sand along this part of the coast is a bit grainier. This was practically powder."

"Like the sand on the beach near the wharf," I said.

Woody's eyes grew. "You're right. That sand is exceptionally fine. It almost seems as if someone hauled it in and put it there."

"It reminds me of the sand on some of the manmade beaches along the gulf, although I'm fairly certain the sand on this particular beach is natural. Still, I suppose the sand from that specific beach could turn out to be a clue."

"That's what I figured. I'm not sure how important it is, but it's a piece of the puzzle. If we can find a few more, a picture may emerge."

"Anything else?" I asked.

"It also occurred to me that I should have told you about the robbery Mr. Oswald called in a week before his murder. I didn't mean to withhold it from you; I just didn't think of it when we spoke."

I brushed my hair behind my ear. "Monica told me about it. Someone stole two books Booker had on his desk. Books that had information about the ship he believed carried the cargo that was donated to the museum."

"That's correct. The theft seemed targeted to me. Mr. Oswald had a fortune in art in his home, yet none of it was taken. Only two books."

I frowned. "From what I understand, the books weren't even one-of-a-kind. It seems whoever stole them could have gotten the information they were after another way. Why go to all the trouble of breaking into a house with a security system to steal them?"

Woody shrugged. "I don't know. It didn't make sense to me at the time and it doesn't make sense now."

"What if someone broke in to steal something of greater value. Something like cash. The alarm went off, so whoever broke in knew they didn't have long before the cops arrived. Maybe they didn't find what they were after, and after scouting out the place a bit, they took the books as a decoy to make it appear as though that was what they were after."

"Could be. The initial break-in could have been a recon mission. Once they got the lay of the land and a peek at the security system, they could have planned to go back to get what they were really after."

I was silent as I tried to figure out a way to let Woody know about Dredge and the fifty grand without sharing the secret of Booker's ghost. I didn't know Woody well enough to be sure how he would react to an announcement of my ability to see ghosts and decided it was best to keep that to myself for now. "I was given some information by a reliable source who prefers to remain unnamed. If I tell you what I know, will you accept that I'm confident that it's solid without requiring me to reveal my source?"

Woody frowned. "Sounds hinky."

"I know. But while I'm at liberty to share the information, I can't reveal the source. Are you interested or not?"

"I'm interested. What do you have?"

"It seems Booker initially hired Oliver Pendergrass to help him look for the sunken ship. Part of his agreement with Pendergrass was that he kept their project to himself. Apparently, Booker was under the impression Pendergrass had talked about it to someone, so he fired him and began looking for a replacement boat and crew. I understand Pendergrass was angry and vowed to 'get what he had coming to him.'"

"So you think Pendergrass killed him?" Woody asked.

"Not necessarily. Let me finish. It gets complicated."

"Okay. I'm listening."

I took a deep breath and then continued. "Booker was given the name of a man who sometimes skirted the line between legal and illegal salvage work. I don't have a real name, but I understand he's called Dredge. On the night he was murdered, Booker met with a representative of this man. Although Booker brought the down payment of fifty thousand dollars with him, he was told the deposit wouldn't be accepted until he was able to offer proof that it was possible to locate the treasure he was after."

Woody frowned. "Mr. Oswald went alone to meet some guy about a job and took fifty grand in cash with him?"

"Yes."

"And you know this how?"

"From my source."

Woody raised a brow. "Of course. Your secret source. Please continue."

"Booker figured he had the proof he needed in the form of the captain's log he'd found decades ago. He didn't have it with him and didn't want to bring Dredge's representative to his home, so he arranged to meet him again the following evening. He took back his money and went home. The cash went into his safe and he changed into his pajamas and robe, then went into the library to look over his charts and graphs. It was while he was doing that that someone broke in and demanded he open the safe. The fifty grand was taken, but the captain's log, also in the safe, was left behind."

"And an anonymous source told you all this?"

I nodded.

"You realize the only people who could possibly know what happened after Booker got home are the man himself and the killer, and the only way the killer could know about the meeting with Dredge's man is if he killed Mr. Oswald?"

"I know. I have to wonder if Dredge's man is the killer. Having said that, I also think it's possible someone other than Dredge's man shot Booker."

"Someone like who?"

I shrugged. "I don't know. But doesn't it feel sort of like a home invasion gone bad?"

"Sure, if this is all fact and not fantasy. There's no way anyone other than Mr. Oswald can know all this, and he's dead. I think your contact is pulling your leg."

"What if Booker was being watched?" Okay, now I was making things up, but the lie seemed to serve my purpose. "What if my source had reason to want to keep an eye on Booker and was following him? What if this individual had put a listening device not only on Booker's person but in his home?"

"Legally?"

I shrugged. "Or not. The point is that the person who provided the information was able to convince me that he could actually see and hear everything that happened."

"Your source is the killer?"

"I didn't say that. I said he was a spy."

Woody leaned back and steepled his fingers. "If this source of yours saw what happened and knew Mr. Oswald was in trouble, why didn't he call 911 when the break-in occurred? If he had, he might have saved his life. Did you think about that?"

"No," I admitted. "I guess I didn't."

"If that was true, if someone was watching him, I think you'd need to tell me who your source is. If you don't, and it turns out this person did kill Mr. Oswald, you could be looking at obstruction charges."

I groaned and took a second to decide what to do. I should have known this would get complicated. I looked at Woody and took a deep breath. "Booker told me what happened."

To his credit, Woody did no more than raise a brow. "Mr. Oswald told you what happened?"

I nodded. "I can see ghosts. I was able to see them when I lived here before too. Now I can speak to them as well. Or at least I can speak to Booker. If you don't believe me, you can ask Mac, Trevor, or Monica. They all know."

Woody didn't say a word. He was probably trying to figure out if he'd been punked.

"I know it's a lot to take in, but I'm not lying. If you don't believe me, come with me to Booker's house and I'll show you."

"Can't Mr. Oswald come here?"

"No. He's bound to the library."

"Okay." Woody stretched the word out. I wondered if his next call would be to mental health. I guess I couldn't blame him for doubting me. "If you can talk to Mr. Oswald, why don't you just ask him who shot him?"

"He doesn't remember. He didn't remember anything past the point where he was at the party at first, but I helped him focus a bit and he could walk me through the evening right up to the point where he was in the library going over his papers and heard a noise. The next thing he remembered was floating over his own body. He didn't remember the money had been taken, but Monica and I checked the safe today and it was gone."

Woody crossed his arms on the table. "You don't seem like a crazy person, but this is a lot to take in."

"I know. I can prove it if you'd like. In fact, I can prove it right now."

"How?"

"Is this office bugged?"

"No."

"There's a spirit in here right now." I glanced at Alyson, who'd come in with me. "I'll leave the room. You say a word. Any word. When I come back, I'll ask the spirit what you said and repeat it back to you."

Woody looked more than just a little doubtful. "Okay. I guess I can do that."

"I'll go out, count to ten, and come back in. Make the word hard. Something I'd never guess."

Woody nodded.

I walked out into the hallway, closing the door behind me. I counted to ten and then returned. Woody was sitting at the table. His face wore a look of doubt, but also curiosity. I looked at Alyson. "Giovanna," I said, repeating what Alyson had told me.

The blood drained from Woody's face. "How did you know that?"

I sat down across from him. "I told you; I can see and speak to ghosts. The ghost in the room agreed to help me out. Do you want to do it again?"

"Yes. Only this time I'll go out. Have the ghost follow me. I'll say something and then come back.'

I nodded to Alyson, who looked as if she was having the most fun ever. When Alyson came back in, she said, "He actually had us go into the bathroom. I guess he figured no bugs in there. The word is Pegasus."

"Really? The bathroom?" I teased. "The word is Pegasus."

Woody's mouth fell open. He dropped into a chair. "Well I'll be."

"Don't worry too much about the ghost thing. The ghost helping me out is a friend who came here with me. I don't sense anyone else lurking around. So, back to Booker. Do you think the real motive for his murder was the money? Could it have been that all along? Might it even have been the motive when whoever broke in the week before the murder and took the books?"

"I have no idea, but robbery of a large amount of cash is as good a motive as any. Let's dig into that angle and see what we can find out."

"Great." I stood up. "The gang is meeting tonight if you want to come over."

"Can you see all ghosts?" Woody asked.

I shook my head. "It's not like I walk around bumping into ghosts all day. The ones I see usually come to me for a reason. Either I'm supposed to help them in some way or they have information I need. The first ghost I saw was Barkley Cutter. I was sixteen and had just moved into his house. He came to me one night, and I knew I had to help him. I found his grandson and helped solve his murder and he moved on. Booker is stuck in the library and wants to move on. I don't think he can until we solve his murder. I intend to help him do just that."

Chapter 13

Monday, May 28

It had been four days since I shared my secret with Woody. Four days since we'd met to try to put a finger on Booker's killer. Four days since I'd learned as much as it appeared I was going to learn from the horse's mouth. I'd visited Booker on two more occasions, but as hard as he appeared to try to push past the limit of his memory of that night, he continued to become stuck at the point at which he heard the noise and looked up. Whatever happened next must have been traumatic. Maybe remembering was simply too difficult a task even for a ghost.

There had been progress in other areas in the past four days. I'd spoken to everyone I even vaguely considered to be a suspect, but everyone seemed to have an alibi, and even those who didn't had no reasonable motive. Logan Poland, the man who'd threatened Booker after he cleaned him out playing poker, had been drinking in a bar on the night of the murder. He not only had a roomful of other patrons to back up his story, he had gone home with a local girl who provided an alibi for the hours after he left the bar. Oliver Pendergrass was as mad as a man can be, and insisted that, despite Booker's demise, the man still owed him money, but he'd been out to sea with another customer when Booker died.

Woody hadn't been able to speak to Dredge. The man was as slippery as an eel, but Woody had asked around and was able to verify that he wasn't the sort to steal from his customers. The more I thought about it, the more certain I was that the reason Booker was blocked was because the killer was someone he knew and trusted. If some random person had shot him, I doubted he'd be suffering the emotional turmoil that appeared to have affected his memory.

On a positive note, my mom confirmed that she'd arranged to fly out with Tucker on Monday of next week. She left her stay open-ended, hinting she planned to stay in Cutter's Cove until I was ready to head home.

That morning, I sat up in my bed and glanced out the window. It was still dark, but I knew the sun was just beyond the horizon. Alyson was sitting in the window seat looking out into the inky blackness, while Sunny and Shadow slept curled up on the bed.

"Who wants to try to catch the sunrise?" I asked.

"I do," Alyson said.

Sunny jumped off the bed and started prancing around, while Shadow yawned and began his morning stretches. I slipped out from beneath the sheets and clicked on my bedside lamp. I pulled on a pair of worn but warm sweatpants and a long-sleeved T-shirt.

Slipping a headband over my hair, I slipped on socks as well as a worn sweatshirt, then tiptoed down the stairs to the kitchen.

After starting the coffee, I pulled on my Nike's, then jotted down a note for Mac, should she rise early and decide to join me. I poured coffee into a large stoneware mug and headed out into the darkness. By the time Alyson, the animals, and I had made it to the bluff, the sky had begun to lighten. Sunny ran around, expending some of the energy she'd gained during the night, while Alyson stood next to me, her hand in mine. Shadow sat at my feet, looking out toward the sea as if he too wanted to be sure to catch the sunrise.

"Wow," Mac said as she walked up next to me.

"Yeah. It's really beautiful."

Mac picked up Shadow and hugged him to her chest. "It's colder than I thought it would be."

"Give it ten minutes. Once the sun pops up over the bluff it will start to warm up. I checked the forecast; it's supposed to be up into the high seventies today."

"Perfect for a day at the beach." Mac grinned.

"I'm really looking forward to this. It's been so long since I committed an entire day to fun."

"You don't have days off from your job?" Mac asked.

"Sure, I have days off. Technically. But I take a lot of work home, and when I'm not working, I'm afraid Ethan tends to make commitments on our behalf that are more work than fun."

Mac glanced at me. "What sort of commitments?"

"He's working his way up the corporate ladder, so he tries to attend all the need-to-be-seen-at parties and social events. I used to think that lifestyle was exactly what I wanted, but now I'm not so sure. What I do know is that I'm a lot more excited about a day at the beach with my friends than I am about attending the June Regatta or some boring yachting party in Newport Ethan keeps trying to convince me to fly home for."

"I suppose yachting could be fun, and there must be a lot of free champagne," Mac mused.

"Trust me, it gets old fast."

"Maybe you should invite Ethan to come out here. Do you think he'd like Cutter's Cove?"

I laughed. "He'd loath everything about it. He'd hate the house, and the early mornings spent watching the sun come up. He'd hate Sunny and Shadow, and if he knew about Alyson, he'd surely have me committed. Ethan's a city boy. He'd be like a fish out of water here."

Mac set Shadow down as the sun peeked over the bluff. "So, I guess what you're saying is that if you marry him someday, visits to Cutter's Cove will most likely be out of the question."

I looked Mac in the eye. "I'm not going to marry Ethan. I'm not sure I'll ever marry anyone. But if I did, it would be someone I could build a life with. Ethan and I have been good for each other. I do care about him and we're compatible in many ways, but I'd be less than honest with myself if I didn't admit we aren't compatible in the most important ways."

The conversation stilled as the sun rose higher in the sky. I stood with my best friend on one side and my other half on the other, and everything felt perfect. Maybe the time had come to have a conversation with Ethan about where our relationship was heading, which, I'd just realized, was nowhere. It was the right thing to do. I planned to be away for another month at least. It seemed fair that I let him go rather than have him wait for me when the end of what we had seemed inevitable now.

"You said Booker heard a noise, looked up, and the next thing he knew, he was dead," Mac said, seemingly out of nowhere.

"Yes. That's what he's been telling me."

"So it seems whoever killed him found their own way into the house."

It took a few seconds, but then a light went on. "I see where you're going with this. Woody said there was no sign of a forced entry, so he's been operating under the assumption that Booker let his killer in, but if Booker is correct and he was sitting alone in the library when someone came in, he hadn't necessarily opened the front door."

"Exactly. I wonder if he remembers setting his alarm."

I turned toward Mac as the sun climbed higher in the sky. "I need to ask him. If he does remember setting the alarm, the killer had to be someone with the alarm code and most likely a key. I'm betting that isn't a very long list."

Mac and I returned to the house. It was a little early to call Monica to ask if it was okay to come over, so I made breakfast while Mac answered some emails. Once the omelets and buttery biscuits were done, I poured us each a glass of orange juice and set everything out on the table on the deck, in the perfect spot to get a panoramic view of the sea.

I texted Trev, telling him to come over to the house whenever he was ready. I wasn't sure how long the interview with Booker would take or if there would be new clues to follow up on once I spoke to him, so it seemed best he come here rather than meeting us at the beach, as we'd discussed last night.

"I'm going to call Monica after we finish eating," I said. "I hate to call too early, but I don't want to risk missing her if she has plans today."

Mac sat down at the table and took a bite of her omelet. "Wow, this is really excellent. What's in it?"

"A few mushrooms, a little bit of fresh spinach, crab, and Havarti cheese. I drizzled a little bit of sour cream sauce, to which I added a pinch of horseradish to give it a bit of a kick."

"It's delicious. And the biscuits look like homemade."

I shrugged. "The recipe is one of my mother's."

"I knew your mom was a great cook, but I had no idea you'd inherited the gene." Mac took another big bite of her omelet, rolling her eyes in pleasure as she chewed.

"I never cook when I'm home in New York. Too busy, I guess. And I don't have the skills my mom does. In fact, I only know how to make a few things she taught me when I still lived at home. But what I do know usually comes out well. And I like to cook. I find it relaxing. I think I'll try out some new recipes while I'm here."

"I volunteer to eat whatever you want to experiment with, and I'm sure Trev will too." Mac finished off her omelet, then took a sip of her coffee. "I'll get the dishes because you cooked. I'll start putting together things for the beach as well."

"Thanks. I'll run upstairs to change into some shorts and then I'll call Monica. It would be so great to have this mystery wrapped up so I can relax and enjoy my time by the sea."

I began to dig through my drawers for appropriate beach attire. I hadn't brought anything quite right for a day lounging around on the sand, but Alyson had left behind bathing suits, cut-off shorts, tank tops, and flip-flops. Choosing a one-piece suit that would work best for surfing, I pulled on a pair of faded cut-off jeans, a yellow tank top, and a dark blue hooded sweatshirt. After slipping my feet into a pair of blue flip-flops, I headed into the bathroom to search for a headband to keep my hair out of my face.

"I'm so excited about today," Alyson said, twirling around the room. "Can Sunny come?"

"We chose a dog beach so she could tag along."

"And Shadow?" Alyson asked.

I glanced at the cat, who was sitting on the bed, watching us chat. "I don't know if he'd like the beach. Cats usually aren't as fond of sand and water as dogs are."

"We can bring a blanket to put under the umbrella. That way he won't have to get wet and sandy if he doesn't want to."

I shrugged. "I'll leave it up to him." I looked at Shadow. "If you want to come, follow us out to the car, and if you don't, I'll be sure your food and water are topped off and you can spend the day here."

"Meow."

I wasn't sure if that was a yes meow, or a thanks-but-no-thanks meow, but Shadow did seem to understand what I'd said, so I figured I'd wait to see whether he showed up at the car.

I grabbed a pile of beach towels, a couple of large blankets, some sunscreen, and a big floppy hat and went downstairs, where Mac had a large picnic basket and an ice chest waiting by the door. I'd left my old surfboard out in the shed, so I hunted around for the key, then went out to fetch it. Mac didn't have her board with her, so Trevor was bringing one for her to use. While in the shed, I grabbed a large beach umbrella and a couple of sand chairs.

When everything was waiting to be loaded into the car, I called Monica. She answered after the second ring. "Amanda. How are you today?"

"I'm good, thank you. We're going to the beach, but I hoped I could swing by to speak to Booker first."

"Absolutely. Any time."

"How about now?"

"Now is fine," Monica confirmed. "It's going to be lovely at the beach. You don't want to waste any more of that sunshine than you have to."

"You're welcome to come along if you like. We're bringing surfboards and we have enough food to stay until after dark."

"Really? You don't think the others will mind?"

"Not at all. You should come. It's going to be a fun, relaxing day."

"Okay. Maybe I will. If you're sure it will be okay with everyone."

"I'm sure. I'll be there in fifteen or twenty minutes."

"I'll get ready for the beach, so just come on in when you get here. I'll meet you in the library."

I headed out to the car, where Alyson, Sunny, and Shadow were waiting for me. The animals should be all right to come along; I only planned to be there for a few minutes. I texted Mac to let her know they were with me and I'd be back as soon as possible.

Unfortunately, that wasn't going to be as soon as I'd thought.

Chapter 14

When I arrived at Booker's I found the front door unlocked, as promised. I went directly down the hallway to the library. I didn't see Booker at first, but when I said his name, his image appeared near the now-dormant fireplace.

"Alyson and Amanda. So good to see you both. Are you here to try to jog my memory again?"

"Actually," I said as I approached him, "I have some different questions for you."

"I'll do my best."

I watched Alyson out of the corner of my eye. She floated over and stood next to Booker. It almost seemed as if she were offering him comfort. "On the night of the murder, you met with Dredge's contact and then came home."

"That's correct."

"When you arrived at the house, was the alarm on?"

Booker answered almost immediately. "It was on. I deactivated it, came in, locked up, and reactivated it before putting the money in the safe and going upstairs to change into my nighttime attire."

"You also said you were sitting at the table here," I placed my hand on it, "when you heard a noise. You looked up and that's the last thing you remember."

Booker nodded. "That's correct. We've gone over all of this before. I'm not sure I can tell you anything new."

"It seems to me that you realized you weren't alone when you saw the person who killed you. If that's true, it seems unlikely you let that person in, as Woody suspected."

Booker frowned. "So how did they get in?"

"Is it possible whoever you saw that night had both a key to the house and the alarm code? Is it possible they let themselves in while you were working in the library?"

Booker shook his head. "That doesn't seem right. The only people with a key and the alarm code are my housekeeper, Monica, and ..." Suddenly, Booker went pale, if it's possible for a ghost to do that, of course.

"And...?" I prompted.

"No. It couldn't be. There has to be another explanation."

I shrugged. "Maybe. But for now, considering anyone who had access to the house seems our best bet."

Booker slipped into a chair. He bent over and rested his head on his knees.

"Booker? Are you all right?" I asked with genuine concern. The man was already dead; I didn't think he could experience any sort of physical harm that in a living person would be associated with shock, but he was certainly feeling emotional distress.

"Who was it, Booker? Who came to see you that night?"

Booker looked up and around the room. "Monica?"

"Monica is the one who came to see you?"

"No, it wasn't Monica." Booker looked around again. "She isn't here?"

I shook my head. "She's upstairs. You remember, don't you? You remember who shot you?"

Booker looked away from me. He stood up and wandered to the window. He looked out into the brilliantly sunny day. "It was Monica's brother, Jessie." Booker turned and looked at me. "You can't tell Monica. It will destroy her."

"But…"

"No. You have to promise me. Monica and Jessie are close despite the fact that she's caring and dependable while her brother is careless and self-centered. If you tell her, it will kill her. I'm already dead. You can't help me, but you can hurt her. Please, I beg of you. We need to keep this to ourselves."

Suddenly, I felt as if I was the one who was trapped. "Booker, she wants to know what happened to you. She needs to know. I don't think she'll let it go until she does know."

"No. Telling her will make things worse."

Oh God. I took a deep breath. "Why don't you tell me exactly what happened?"

Booker began to float around the room in a seemingly meaningless manner. Ghost pacing again, I assumed. "I heard a noise and looked up. It was Jessie. He had come earlier, while I was at the party.

He'd let himself in, reset the alarm, and then helped himself to my liquor cabinet. I think his original intention was simply to go up to a guest room and wait to speak to me the following day, but apparently, the alcohol made him both angry and careless, and he came down to the library." Booker paused. I was pretty sure ghosts couldn't cry, but if it was possible, that's what he would have been doing.

"Go on," I encouraged.

"At first, I was happy to see him, but then I realized how drunk he was. Jessie is a sweet kid most of the time and we usually got along just fine, but he's a mean drunk. I tried to make small talk, but he started right in by insisting that I needed to give him some money. A lot of it. I told him I wasn't going to turn over the amount of cash he wanted without a serious conversation about what he needed it for, and I wasn't going to have that conversation while he was drunk. That seemed to enrage him. The next thing I knew, he was waving a gun around, insisting I favored Monica. He accused me of loving her more, even though he was blood, the same as her. He said I seemed to be willing to help her out whenever she needed money, while I turned him down time after time."

Booker sat down abruptly. I waited until he was ready to speak again.

"Jessie was so angry," Booker continued. "I should have realized and done more to diffuse the situation; instead, I tried to explain my side of things, while he went on and on about getting his share and making things right. I tried to talk him into giving me the gun and going back to bed, but he was like a wild man. I should have known the danger in mixing alcohol and suppressed rage and given him what he wanted, but I didn't."

"But the money was missing. If you didn't give it to him, what happened to it?" I asked.

"I didn't die right away. After Jessie shot me, he seemed to be in shock. I told him to call for help, but he said he wouldn't do that unless I gave him the money he was after. I gave him the combination to the safe. He took the money and left. I hoped he'd call 911 once he was safely away from the house, but I guess he didn't."

"I'm so very sorry." A tear slid down my cheek. "I can't even imagine how hard this is for you, but I need to tell Woody that Jessie is the one who shot you."

Booker shook his head. "No. You can't. There's no reason to destroy any more lives."

I turned away to try to gather my thoughts, which was when I saw Monica standing in the doorway. She looked as if she'd seen a ghost, but I didn't think that was the case. She must have heard what I'd just said to Booker.

"Jessie shot Uncle Rory?" she asked in a voice so soft I barely heard her.

I crossed the room and pulled her into my arms. "I'm so sorry. I should have been more careful about what I said. Booker didn't want you to know, and while I felt you should be told, I certainly didn't want you to find out this way."

Monica squeezed me back, then took a step back. "It's all right. I should have known."

"You knew Jessie was here?"

Monica shook her head. "No. But I knew he needed money to pay off a gambling debt. He'd been after me for days to give him what I had, but I refused. I'd helped him out so many times, and each time he'd promise to stop, but he never did. I called him after I heard about Uncle Rory. He acted all cool and unaffected, but that was Jessie after he'd been drinking. I was dealing with my own grief, so I let it go. When he made a comment about being his own family and taking care of himself because no one who shared his blood cared about what he was going through, I just thought he was having one of his episodes."

"Episodes?"

"Jessie not only has problems with alcohol, he has problems with depression. He makes bad decisions. Really bad decisions. I know that's why Uncle Rory didn't want to leave us the house. I didn't blame him." A tear slid down Monica's cheek. She wiped it away with the back of her hand. "When we discovered Uncle Rory's money was missing, I should have put two and two together immediately. I should have known the only reason Jessie wasn't sniffing around, hoping Uncle Rory had left me money I could lend him, was because he'd already acquired what he needed."

"Tell Monica we don't have to call Woody. Tell her that we can keep this between us," Booker said.

I glanced at him and frowned.

"Tell her," he insisted.

"What is it? Is Uncle Rory saying something?" Monica asked.

I repeated what Booker had said.

She slowly shook her head as tears slid down her cheeks. "No. We have to tell. Jessie needs help. He killed his own blood. And he doesn't seem to feel any remorse." Monica looked at me. "We need to tell what we know. Will you make the call?"

I glanced at where Booker had been standing, but he'd faded away. "Yes," I said turning back to Monica. "I'll make the call."

Chapter 15

By the time I'd gotten hold of Woody, explained exactly what had occurred and how I knew it, and he'd put out an all-points bulletin on Jessie, it was well in to the afternoon. Mac had come by to pick up the animals, who were waiting in the car for me. I told her to go on ahead to the beach with Trevor and the animals and I'd meet them there when I was done at Booker's house.

I wasn't sure where Booker and Alyson had gone off to. I imagined she was trying to comfort him. Monica seemed to want to be alone, so when Woody released me, I drove to the beach. Part of me felt as if it was wrong to try to salvage what was left of the day, but another knew I'd done all I could, and hanging around wasn't helping anyone.

The first sixty minutes at the beach I spent catching Mac and Trevor up on what had happened, but after that, what I really needed was some time alone on the water. I pulled on my sweatshirt and paddled out beyond the breakers. Once I was out far enough, I just sat on my board and floated.

I felt so bad for both Booker and Monica. They both cared for Jessie despite his weaknesses, and she would suffer greatly as she watched Jessie go through what was going to be the most difficult time in his life. I knew I wouldn't be able to stand it if anyone I loved ended up in prison, but Monica hadn't been wrong when she'd recognized her brother needed help, and maybe he'd get it there.

I hoped Booker would move on now that his murder was solved. I'd had a chance to connect with him again for a time, and I'd miss him when he passed over, but the goal of a pure and unencumbered spirit was to do just that. I suspected Alyson would help with that. She had a purity and compassion I knew I didn't have as Amanda, and I realized that by finding a way to join the parts of us, I wouldn't simply be eliminating a pest, but would be reclaiming the very best parts of myself, which I seemed to have lost along the way.

After a while, I felt I'd decompressed enough, so I picked a wave and surfed back to shore. When I arrived, Trevor had the fire going and Mac had begun to unpack the picnic. Sunny was laying on the blanket next to Shadow. It appeared both had decided to take a nap in the shade. There was still no sign of Alyson. I wasn't entirely sure she could get here on her own. Perhaps I should drive back to Booker's to see if she needed a ride.

"Feeling better?" Trevor asked after kissing me on the cheek.

"Much. I'm sorry about the way things worked out, but I'm glad Booker's killer will be brought to justice."

"I feel so bad for Monica," Mac said. "Her brother is her only family now that Booker is dead."

I grabbed a handful of potato chips. "Me too. She was incredibly brave today. Booker didn't want me to tell Woody what happened to him."

"Would you really have kept such a big secret?" Mac asked.

"Honestly? I have no idea. I was really struggling with it when Monica saved my having to make the decision by announcing she'd overheard part of the conversation I was having with Booker."

"The next few weeks, even the next few months, are going to be really hard for her. We should make it a point to include her in whatever we decide to do," Mac said. "Assuming you plan to stick around for a while, now that the mystery you came here for is solved."

"I do plan to stick around. Mom is coming next week, and I know she's excited to spend some time here. I have almost five weeks left on the leave I took from work, and I plan to use every one of those days, How about you? Can you stay?"

Mac nodded. "I'd like that very much."

I glanced at Trevor. "Then it's settled. Trev will just have to put up with having us underfoot for a while longer."

"Trust me," Trevor smiled, "I'm happy to have you underfoot for as long as you can stay." He put an arm around each of us. "I missed you guys. More than you'll never know."

I was about to respond when Sunny jumped up and took off across the sand to the parking lot. I glanced in that direction and saw Monica crossing the sand with Alyson trotting along beside her. I didn't think Monica could see her, or that she even knew of her existence, so I had to assume Monica had decided to come out to the beach as originally planned and Alyson had hitched a ride.

"Monica, I'm so glad you came." Mac hugged her.

"Once they found Jessie and arrested him, I figured there was no reason for me to sit in that huge house being sad when I had friends waiting for me at the beach." Monica looked at me. "I don't know if Uncle Rory is still in the house or if he's moved on. Perhaps you can stop by and let me know."

"I'd be happy to. Any time."

"Will you be going home now?"

"No. I think I'll stay a while. I've only just gotten here, and I did take a six-week leave from work. Besides, my mom is coming next week."

Monica wrapped me in a tight hug. "Thank you."

I hugged Monica in return as I watched Alyson and Sunny playing on the sand over her shoulder. It had been a difficult and emotional week, but darn if it wasn't good to be home again.

NEXT FROM
KATHI DALEY BOOKS

https://amzn.to/2GxKau1

Preview of Chapter 1

Thursday, May 3

They arrived in the middle of the night. Two balls of wet and matted fur tied to a porch railing, huddled together for warmth and comfort as the rain slammed into the small town of White Eagle, Montana, from the east. The note said they were inseparable, brothers who'd shared a womb and eventually a life. Neither had spent time without the other, and, the anonymous person who'd dropped them on Brady's doorstep asked, if at all possible, could they be placed together?

Placing dogs with just the right owner was a task Brady Baker, local veterinarian and shelter owner, and I, Tess Thomas, mail carrier and shelter volunteer, take great pride in doing it better than anyone else, but this pair of medium-sized terriers were proving to be quite a challenge. It wasn't that they weren't adorable, with their huge brown eyes and long shaggy fur the color of damp sand, it was that they had never been trained or socialized to respond to or even care about anyone or anything other than each other.

And then they met Tilly.

"It looks like you're making progress."

Brady smiled in response to my statement as my golden retriever, Tilly, and I walked into the room where he'd been working on a sit/stay with one of the brothers. It appeared as if the training had been going well until Jagger saw Tilly. Ignoring Brady's command to stay, he'd run forward to greet her with wiggles and waggles from one end of his shaggy body to the other.

I motioned for Tilly to sit, which she did immediately. Jagger, who Brady estimated to be about eight months old, plopped his butt on the ground right next to her. I praised them both and told them to stay. I walked away and spoke to Brady for a minute, keeping an eye on the pair as I did. After a minute, I motioned for the dogs to come and then sit and stay again. I asked both Jagger and Tilly to repeat the behavior several times, praising both dogs when my hand gesture was met with an appropriate response. When a dog was in training, repetition was key. Experience had shown that if a behavior was repeated often enough, even easily distractible dogs such as Jagger would begin to respond to the hand flip even when Tilly wasn't around to show him what to do.

Once I'd released them to relax, Jagger came over to say hi. I knelt to greet the terrier and was welcomed with wet, sloppy kisses. The fact that Jagger now seemed delighted to see me when he'd all but ignored me in those first days was progress in my book.

"Where's Bowie?" I asked about the second terrier.

"In his pen," Brady answered as his blue eyes met my brown. "I've decided the only way I'm going to make any progress training the boys is to separate them for individual sessions. Initially, I tried joint sessions, but that wasn't getting me anywhere. I figure once I have them responding individually, I can bring them together for training for short periods of time." Brady bent over and greeted Tilly, allowing her to enthusiastically rain doggy kisses on his face.

"Seems like you have a good plan. How can I help?"

"I'm glad you asked. I hoped you and Tilly would have time to work with the brothers and me on Saturday. Between the clinic and the shelter, it's hard to make time for the specialty training they need. Besides, Tilly is a good influence on Bowie and Jagger. They seem to settle down and pay more attention when she's with them."

Brady had a point. Tilly was an old pro at responding to both hand and verbal signals. When she was around, Jagger and Bowie tended to mimic whatever she was doing.

"Tilly and I would be happy to help," I answered. "Did you have anything specific in mind?" Brady interviewed prospective doggy parents to find out exactly what they were looking for in a dog. He wanted to ensure that the dogs he placed were perfect matches for their new humans. If the shelter housed a dog who seemed to be compatible overall with one of the humans who came looking for a forever friend, more often than not, Brady was willing to provide extra training to ensure the dog met the specific needs of whoever they'd spend their life with.

"I spoke to Jimmy Early. He came in to adopt one dog, but after we spoke, he said he'd be willing to consider the brothers provided they loved the water, were comfortable on a SUP board, and enjoyed traveling."

I knew Jimmy. He and his girlfriend, Destiny, operated a paddleboat and stand up paddle board concession at the lake during the spring and summer. Once the snow began to fall, they packed up their belongings and took off in their camper for warmer climes. It made sense they'd want to adopt dogs who liked the water and travel. "Have you tried the boys in the water?"

Brady nodded. "They aren't fans of the wet stuff. Tilly likes to swim. Maybe we can take the boys to the beach on Saturday and Tilly can show them how much fun it is. Once we get them used to the water, we can work on the SUP board. As for traveling, they seem fine riding around in my truck, so I don't think that will be a problem."

"Okay. I can do Saturday. Say around ten?"

"Ten would be perfect."

I paused to put the appointment in my phone calendar. "The reason I'm here now," I said, once I'd finished the entry, "is because I wanted to pick up some more of that nutrient-dense cat food for the kittens." I had adopted two rescues of my own, an orange-stripped kitten named Tang and a black kitten with long fur named Tinder. As a shelter volunteer, I was able to purchase quality pet food at Brady's cost, so it was only the best that my discount, combined with my adequate-but-far-from-generous salary could buy for my animals.

"I was about to quit for the day," Brady informed me. "Let me bring Jagger back to his brother and I'll go to the clinic with you. You can grab the food as well as the flyers I had made up for the adoption event later this month."

I followed Brady, who was dressed in faded jeans, running shoes, and a dark blue T-shirt. He dressed in slacks, a dress shirt, and a white lab coat when the clinic was open, but when he spent time at the shelter, he dressed down, which was the look I appreciated the most. "Did you decide on a theme for the event?"

Brady's eyes lit up with enthusiasm. "Speed dating. I've arranged to use the football field at the high school. I'm going to section it off into twelve smaller areas using temporary fencing. Each individual pen will have a dog who's available for adoption. Prospective doggy parents will each be assigned to a pen, where they'll spend three minutes. When the time's up, all the people will rotate in a prearranged pattern until everyone has visited all the pens. Once a prospective doggy parent has their visit with each of the twelve dogs, they'll be able to request up to three dogs to spend additional time with. At the end of the event, prospective parents can fill out an application for the dog of their choice."

"Are you going to allow for second and third choices just in case everyone wants the same dog?" It seemed that at almost every adoption clinic I'd ever worked, there were interested parties fighting over a few dogs, while others remained homeless.

He nodded. "Some prospective parents don't do well with this sort of event, and they're of course welcome to come in during the week to look at the dogs individually, but I've done speed-dating events before, and usually, dogs and humans manage to find one another in the time allotted."

"Sounds like fun. I'll start putting the flyers up tomorrow while I'm doing my route."

"If you need more, just ask and I can run some out to you. I want this event to be a success, and I'm hoping we're starting early enough this time to plaster the entire town."

"I'll make sure every bulletin board and store window in White Eagle has a flyer."

I got the cat food and flyers from Brady's veterinary clinic, and Tilly and I piled into my Jeep and headed home: a small, rustic cabin outside the town limits of White Eagle. While the plumbing was old and the heater temperamental, the view of the mountains from both my front and back decks was truly spectacular. The cabin was surrounded by national forest and my closest neighbor was far enough away that I couldn't see any other buildings from any window.

When I pulled into the private drive that led from the highway to the cabin, I spotted my good friend

Tony Marconi sitting in his truck in front of the cabin. Tony and I had met in middle school. He was not only the smartest kid in our entire school, but he was also sort of a geek. I'll admit that when I first met him, I, like the other kids, had made fun of his looks and superior intellect, but after he helped me out with a mystery that resulted in the two of us sharing a pretty huge secret, the tall and gangly genius had grown on me and eventually become one of my very best friends.

Of course, now that he was an adult and had grown into his height, he was not only the smartest man I knew but the sexiest as well. Not that I would *ever* tell him that. We were, after all, just friends.

"What are you doing here?" I asked as I climbed out of the Jeep and Tony kissed me on the cheek. "Not that I'm not thrilled to see you; I just wasn't expecting you."

"I was in town and thought I'd stop by to see if you wanted to have a pizza and video game night. It's been a while."

"It has been a while," I answered as Tilly jumped out of the Jeep and greeted Tony's dog, Titan, with a wagging tail and tiny leaps of joy. "And I don't have plans tonight. I wish I'd known what you had in mind. I would have stopped to pick up the food on my way home."

"No need. I have a pizza warming in your oven and a new microbrew I've been wanting to try in your refrigerator."

After Titan greeted Tilly, he trotted over to say hi to me, while Tilly greeted Tony. "If you had a way into the cabin, why were you waiting out here in your truck?"

"It seemed presumptuous to wait inside. I knew you probably wouldn't be long, it's a beautiful evening, and you do have quite the spectacular view here."

I ruffled Titan behind the ears, then kissed him on the top of the head. "I'm glad you're here, but you probably should have called. What if I wasn't free?"

Tony shrugged as Tilly and Titan headed to my front door together. "I would have taken my beer and pizza home. Let me just grab a few things from my truck and I'll get the game set up."

"Do you have a new one?"

"I do. It's called Valley of Atonement. I've been asked to test if for a friend. You can help."

One of the very best things about Tony, second to his good looks, giving nature, kind heart, millions of dollars, and superior brain, was that he knew a lot of people who developed video games and was always being asked to test them and offer advice before they were on the market. Most of the time he asked me and his other friend, Shaggy, to test them out as well.

"I hope you didn't order pineapple on the pizza," I said as I walked to the door with Tony trailing behind me.

"I would never get pineapple on any pizza I planned to share with you. There are also no mushrooms, peppers, or tomatoes. All meat, all the way."

I grinned. "Thanks. I know you love pineapple on your pizza, so I appreciate the sacrifice. Why don't you set everything up while I change out of my work clothes?" As a mail carrier I had a uniform I was required to wear every day, but when I was home, it was sweatpants, jeans, or shorts.

I greeted both kittens and headed into my bedroom, where I put on a pair of jeans and a T-shirt. I pulled my long hair into a ponytail, then returned to the main living area of the cabin, where Tony had the pizza on the table, along with plates, forks, and ice-cold beer. It was a beautiful day and I was tempted to move the dinner outdoors onto my deck, but it was still a little chilly in the evenings, although the snow had melted and the meadows were lush with green grass and colorful wildflowers.

"This really is the best pizza in town," I said as I took my first bite of the thickly layered pie.

"Having Giovani's Pizza on a regular basis is one of the things I miss about living closer to town," Tony said. "I noticed they had a few new specialties, including a buffalo chicken topping that sounds like it might be fun to try."

"That does sound good. We'll have to try it next time." I slipped a second piece of pizza onto my plate. "Shaggy loves chicken wings, so I'm betting he'd like to try it as well." Shaggy, who owned a video game store, and the two spent quite a bit of time together. "I'm surprised you didn't bring him with him tonight."

"I thought about inviting him, but I wanted to talk to you about something."

I set my slice down. "My dad?"

Tony had been trying to help me track down my father, who supposedly died twelve years ago. For some reason, I had a feeling there was more to his death than I'd been told, so I'd asked Tony to look in to it. Not only had he found what seemed like proof that Dad hadn't died in the fiery accident, as everyone thought, but there was every indication that he could still be alive and living an alternate life.

"No, not your dad," Tony said.

"Okay." I couldn't imagine what Tony would want to discuss with me that he wouldn't want Shaggy to overhear if it wasn't regarding my father and his not-so-dead state of being. "Then what is it?"

Tony paused and made eye contact before he continued. Okay, he was making me nervous now. It wasn't like Tony to hesitate. I watched as a myriad of emotions crossed his face. Eventually, he spoke. "Remember you asked me to check out the man who came to White Eagle to visit your mother over Valentine's Day?"

"I remember. His name is Romero Montenegro. He lives in Italy, where his family owns a winery. You said he checked out. You said he used to work in a museum but now teaches history at a university in Rome, although he's been on sabbatical. You said he'd never been married or arrested, though he did have one failed engagement seven years ago. You said he seemed like a good guy. Did you find something else?"

Tony hesitated. Oh, I didn't like the look on his face. Tony was the sort who was always confident and sure. This look of doubt and indecision didn't fit him at all.

"What is it?" I asked in a much firmer tone.

"Is your mom still seeing him?" Tony asked.

"He went back to Italy, so I guess she isn't technically seeing him, but they're still corresponding. She's even made some noises to Ruthie and me about taking some time off over the summer so she can travel to Italy to visit him. I've been trying to talk her out of it. I mean, she's fifty-six and the mother of two adults, and he's a forty-two-year-old playboy. I don't see what she sees in the man. They have absolutely nothing in common."

Tony raised an eyebrow. I knew what he wasn't saying. Romero was a total babe in a cover-of-a-romance-novel way. Dark and fit, with a polished air and a wonderful accent. Of course my middle-aged mother would find him attractive. She'd have to be dead not to be. But sizzling-hot sex appeal wasn't everything. Though in Romero's case, it might be enough.

"Do you think we can move on from this line of thought?" I asked. "The idea of my mother feeling those type of feelings sort of grosses me out."

"I guess I can understand that."

"So, what's the deal? Why are we even discussing the Casanova who's gained my mother's attention?"

Tony splayed his hands on the table, his long fingers open wide. "I'm not sure why I even continued to look into his past after that initial search, but something felt off, so when I had some free time, I poked around a bit more. Remember I told you that Romero hadn't been married but he'd had a failed engagement seven years ago?"

"Yeah. So?"

"It looks like the guy didn't break up with his fiancée and she didn't break up with him."

I sat back in my chair and crossed my arms over my chest. "Okay, what are you saying? Is the guy my mom has been fooling around with still engaged?"

"No. He's not engaged. Romero Montenegro didn't get married because his engagement failed. The reason he didn't get married was because his fiancée died. She was, in fact, murdered."

Books by Kathi Daley
Come for the murder, stay for the romance.

Zoe Donovan Cozy Mystery:
Halloween Hijinks
The Trouble With Turkeys
Christmas Crazy
Cupid's Curse
Big Bunny Bump-off
Beach Blanket Barbie
Maui Madness
Derby Divas
Haunted Hamlet
Turkeys, Tuxes, and Tabbies
Christmas Cozy
Alaskan Alliance
Matrimony Meltdown
Soul Surrender
Heavenly Honeymoon
Hopscotch Homicide
Ghostly Graveyard
Santa Sleuth
Shamrock Shenanigans
Kitten Kaboodle
Costume Catastrophe
Candy Cane Caper
Holiday Hangover
Easter Escapade
Camp Carter
Trick or Treason
Reindeer Roundup
Hippity Hoppity Homicide

Zimmerman Academy The New Normal
Ashton Falls Cozy Cookbook

Tj Jensen Paradise Lake Mysteries by Henery Press:

Pumpkins in Paradise
Snowmen in Paradise
Bikinis in Paradise
Christmas in Paradise
Puppies in Paradise
Halloween in Paradise
Treasure in Paradise
Fireworks in Paradise
Beaches in Paradise – *July 2018*

Whales and Tails Cozy Mystery:

Romeow and Juliet
The Mad Catter
Grimm's Furry Tail
Much Ado About Felines
Legend of Tabby Hollow
Cat of Christmas Past
A Tale of Two Tabbies
The Great Catsby
Count Catula
The Cat of Christmas Present
A Winter's Tail
The Taming of the Tabby
Frankencat
The Cat of Christmas Future
Farewell to Felines
The Cat of New Orleans – *June 2018*

Writers' Retreat Southern Seashore Mystery:

First Case
Second Look
Third Strike
Fourth Victim
Fifth Night
Sixth Cabin – *May 2018*

Rescue Alaska Paranormal Mystery:

Finding Justice
Finding Answers – *May 2018*

A Tess and Tilly Mystery:

The Christmas Letter
The Valentine Mystery
The Mother's Day Mishap – *April 2018*

Sand and Sea Hawaiian Mystery:

Murder at Dolphin Bay
Murder at Sunrise Beach
Murder at the Witching Hour
Murder at Christmas
Murder at Turtle Cove
Murder at Water's Edge
Murder at Midnight

Haunting by the Sea:

Homecoming by the Sea

Seacliff High Mystery:

The Secret
The Curse
The Relic
The Conspiracy
The Grudge
The Shadow
The Haunting

Road to Christmas Romance:

Road to Christmas Past

USA Today best-selling author Kathi Daley lives in beautiful Lake Tahoe with her husband Ken. When she isn't writing, she likes spending time hiking the miles of desolate trails surrounding her home. She has authored more than seventy-five books in eight series, including Zoe Donovan Cozy Mysteries, Whales and Tails Island Mysteries, Sand and Sea Hawaiian Mysteries, Tj Jensen Paradise Lake Series, Writers' Retreat Southern Seashore Mysteries, Rescue Alaska Paranormal Mysteries, and Seacliff High Teen Mysteries. Find out more about her books at **www.kathidaley.com**

Stay up to date:

Newsletter, *The Daley Weekly* **http://eepurl.com/NRPDf**
Kathi Daley Blog – publishes each Friday
http://kathidaleyblog.com
Webpage – **www.kathidaley.com**
Facebook at Kathi Daley Books –
www.facebook.com/kathidaleybooks
Kathi Daley Books Group Page –
https://www.facebook.com/groups/569578823146850/
E-mail – **kathidaley@kathidaley.com**
Twitter at Kathi Daley@kathidaley –
https://twitter.com/kathidaley
Amazon Author Page –
https://www.amazon.com/author/kathidaley
BookBub – **https://www.bookbub.com/authors/kathi-daley**
Pinterest – **http://www.pinterest.com/kathidaley/**

89618009R00108

Made in the USA
Middletown, DE
17 September 2018